WOODROW'S LAST HEIST

Woodrow Liddell, the last of the old heisters, just out of San Quentin pen after a fifteen-year stretch, tries out his old skills again by robbing a Canadian Pacific flyer's strongbox. Bob Helman and his gang, who were in on the raid, double-cross Woodrow and take off with all the cash. Woodrow, shot by Helman, was left for dead in the mail-car. But he recovers and sets out on his vengeance trail . . .

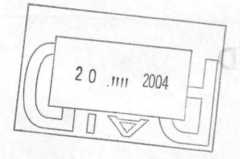

Books by Elliot Conway
in the Linford Western Library:

THE MAVERICK
THE LONER
THE PEACE OFFICER
THE BLUE-BELLY SERGEANT

ELLIOT CONWAY

WOODROW'S LAST HEIST

Complete and Unabridged

LINFORD
Leicester

First published in Great Britain in 1996 by
Robert Hale Limited
London

First Linford Edition
published 1997
by arrangement with
Robert Hale Limited
London

The right of Elliot Conway to be
identified as the author of this work has
been asserted by him in accordance with the
Copyright, Designs and Patents Act, 1988

British Library CIP Data

Conway, Elliot
    Woodrow's last heist.—Large print ed.—
Linford western library
    1. Western stories
    2. Large type books
    I. Title
    823.9′14 [F]

    ISBN 0–7089–5136–8

Published by
F. A. Thorpe (Publishing) Ltd.
Anstey, Leicestershire
Set by Words & Graphics Ltd.
Anstey, Leicestershire
Printed and bound in Great Britain by
T. J. International Ltd., Padstow, Cornwall

This book is printed on acid-free paper

For Liz and Una
who have made the big time

1

THE white haired elderly man, in a dark-coloured store suit, felt the speed of the train dropping as the big Canadian Pacific trans-continental loco, smoke and sparks belching from its stack, hit the beginning of the twelve mile twisting and looping grade of Long Haul Pass. The time had arrived to put the weeks of planning into action.

He got up from his seat, touching the brim of his high-crowned plains hat to the two middle-aged ladies sitting opposite him.

"I'm just stepping outside for a spell, ladies," he said. He smiled. "To have my evening cigar. Then I won't bother you with the smoke." His smile took on a saddened look. "My doctor only allows me one cigar a day on account of my chest complaint."

"Why that's right gentlemanly of

you, sir, isn't it, Mabel?" one of the matrons said.

"It is Dulcie," her friend replied. Then looking up at the elderly man she added, "but you needn't do so. We wouldn't want you get cold standing out there on the platform on our behalf, would we, Dulcie."

"We sure wouldn't, Mabel," said Dulcie.

"I'll take care, I won't stay out long," the elderly man said. Which was as big a lie as any the elderly man had told before. And in his life as a stage and bank heister, Woodrow Liddell had told more than a few. If things went according to plan the old ladies would never gaze on his face again. He would be ass-kicking it down through the snows of the high ridges to the State border with the money shipment from the baggage car strong box packed in the saddle-bags of the Liddell gang.

Woodrow strode along the centre aisle to the rear door of the car with a straight-backed determination that belied the fact that he was coming up to his seventieth birthday. It had been over sixteen years since he had pulled his last heist, long ways south of here, in New Mexico. That one, along with the payroll the Wells Fargo stage had been carrying, had netted him a twenty-year sentence in San Quentin, serving fifteen of them before being paroled. That long stretch behind bars had in no way dampened his enthusiasm and confidence in being able to pull a heist and stay out of the law's hands so that he could enjoy the proceeds of the caper. After all, he thought, a man's got to do what he's best at.

Though he had to admit, having rubbed shoulders with the best of his calling, the James and the Younger boys, and several hard-nosed loners, the four pinched-assed-visaged, hair-triggered-dispositioned youths he had rounded up to pull off the raid, weren't up to his standards of men to walk the line with, or even have a casual drink with at some bar if he was being really critical. But there again, all the old, experienced hands were dead, killed in shoot-outs with the law, or rotting in some State Pen, so he had to make do with the only hired help available.

Woodrow opened the door and stepped out on to the narrow platform, swaying with the motion of the train, closing the door behind him. Across the wind-tugging gap, a tall man's stride away, was the door of the baggage car, and the money. And the three armed guards. Woodrow thin-smiled. He'd faced bigger odds and come through OK. He ignored the small voice in his head telling him that he'd aged a heap since then and that his foolish pride in thinking that he wasn't an over-the- hill old fart, hadn't lost any of his skill, was leading him up Shit Creek.

He heard the door open again and three men crowded on to the platform alongside him. His hired help had arrived. He gave each of them a hard-eyed bossman's look.

"Remember boys," he grated, "we do it my way, slowly and easily, then we'll pull it off without anyone getting hurt. The sonsuvbitches will raise a hunt for us as it is; any killin' on our part then it will be a real big hunt. State marshals, mounties, Pinkertons, even bounty-hunters, attracted by the price on our hides, will join in the chase. This is my last heist and I want to be able to live out the rest of my life in peace with my cut. I sure don't want to spend it ass-kickin' a few hours ahead of some hangin' posse."

The tallest of the trio, a thin-shouldered, weasel-eyed youth, favoured Woodrow with a sneering grin. "As long as those guys in that car," he said, pointing across the gap, "wear kid gloves we'll wear ours. Ain't that right, boys? Now let's get this show on the road, old man, before Jose waiting at the head of the pass with the horses has his balls frozen off."

Old man. Woodrow stiffened with anger. Christ, he was robbing stages when the bastard was only a lustful look in his future pa's eyes. It would give him great pleasure, after the job was done, to bend his Colt over Helman's head to knock the cockiness out of him. He was the loud-mouth of the four, favouring wearing two guns. Boasted to the others that he had killed two men in Colorado. Backshot them from some dark alley, Woodrow professionally opined. But, he thought, every man has a cross to bear, and the four assholes he'd hired were his.

"Wait here," he said curtly, "'till I see to the guard at the door." Then he stepped over on to the platform of the baggage car and rapped on the door. He blocked the guard's vision peering at him through the wire-meshed glass panel from seeing the men behind him.

Woodrow heard the rattle of bolts being withdrawn and the door was opened a few inches, still being held by a heavy-linked safety chain, though wide enough for him to see a hand pointing a big pistol at his belly.

"What do you want, mister?" the guard barked, still not fully showing himself. "Passengers don't collect their bags till we make a regular stop, and then only by the platform door."

"I know that," replied Woodrow, apologetic-voiced. "But I've left my cigars in my trunk and I'm kinda craving for a smoke. It won't take more than a couple minutes. You and your buddies will be welcome to have one. They're genuine Havana."

Woodrow waited, all screwed up inside. In spite of what he had told Helman about the way he wanted to play it, it could still turn out into a bloody gun battle. His hand in his right coat pocket gripped the pistol butt harder. His tension eased somewhat when the guard said, albeit reluctantly, "OK then, but be quick. As I said, it's against company rules for passengers to come into the baggage car when the train's on the move."

Woodrow laughed. "I ain't after what

you must be carryin' in the railroad safe, mister. Not when you and your two buddies are in there all armed up. All I want is my cigars."

The door closed again and Woodrow heard the safety chain being loosened then the door fully opened. By the light from the baggage car lanterns the guard saw the three men on the opposite platform. Woodrow leaned in the car and jabbed his pistol hard in the guard's stomach, before the alarm he had seen mirrored in his face could be transmitted into a warning shout to the other two guards. He eased the pistol out of the guard's unresisting fingers and hard-voiced hissed, "One yelp outa you, pilgrim, and I'll ventilate your hide, and that's a fact." He emphasized that ominous fact by boring the muzzle of the Colt deeper into the guard's soft fleshy belly. The only sound the guard made was a low gasp of pain. "Now, walk back along the car to the other two as though everything is OK," Woodrow ordered.

With Woodrow's pistol now pressing hard in his back the guard felt that he had no other option but to do what the hard-faced son-of-a-bitch had told him to do, unless he wanted a quick death. The other two guards, sitting on crates playing a hand of poker, gave them a casual glance then carried on with their game. Getting close up to them Woodrow tugged at his hostage's sleeve to draw him to a halt.

Conversationally he said, "Gents, this is a heist. Go for those pistols you're wearin' and you'll get your buddy well and truly dead. You sit there and finish your game then no one need get hurt." Woodrow smiled at them. "But before you do whoever of you has the keys to the safe I'd be right obliged if you'd hand them over."

The two guards sat unmoving as though carved from wood, taking in their white-faced buddy and the old man holding the pistol in his ribs, weighing up their chances of getting the drop on the heister. After all, although he had the edge now, it was still three to one in their favour. The old man had only to drop his guard for a second. Three more pistol-wielding men bursting into the car quickly dispelled any possible moves that they had been comtemplating. The railroad didn't pay them enough to risk committing suicide.

"You ain't got a chance," Woodrow said, guessing what had been going through their minds. "So let's keep it peaceful as I said. Now hand over the keys to the safe; me and my boys are runnin' a tight schedule."

One of the card players after taking a quick, forlorn-hope glance at the rifle leaning up against a nearby crate reached up and lifted a key-ring with two keys dangling from it from a nail in the side of the car above his head and handed it to Woodrow.

Woodrow smiled at him. "Good, you're bein' right sensible." He stuffed his pistol back into the waistband of his pants and kneeling down at the safe inserted the keys in the twin locks, beaming with satisfaction as he heard the dull clicks of the locking levers sliding free. He swung the door wide open and his beam broadened into a big full-faced smile. "The pot at the end of the Goddamned rainbow, boys," he breathed. "I told you it would be like money from home." He lifted the tightly banded stacks of bills out of the safe and began stuffing them into an empty mailbag lying beside his feet. "One of you slip the cuffs on the guards," he said. "And fasten them to that big crate so that they can't get to the emergency brake cord when we depart. I'll open the side door then we're ready to jump off as soon as we see Jose's signal fire."

"I ain't leavin' three men breathin' who can describe our likeness to the law, old man," Herman said.

Before Woodrow could tell him that he had only brought him and his three men in on the raid on the stated understanding that there would be no killings, Helman's pistol flashed and roared in three quick shots and the guards fell to the floor to lie in unmoving, twisted-limbed heaps.

"You murderous sonuvabitch!" Woodrow yelled and leaped to his feet, drawing his gun.

Helman wolf-smiled back at him and fired a fourth shot as the train rocked and swayed its way through a sharp dog-leg bend. Woodrow felt as though a red-hot branding iron had struck him heavily on the left temple and blacked-out, dropping alongside the dead guards, lying as still as them.

Helman turned him over on to his back with his foot and saw the blood streaming from Woodrow's head wound. "The old has-been only got downed a mite early, boys," he said. "There was no way I was goin' to let him keep his cut." He grinned. "He's too old to enjoy spendin' it. Though to be fair to the old goat he sure knew how to set a train heist. Zeb, get that door open and keep an eye out for Jose's fire, we must be gettin' close to the head of the pass. You, Stu, finish putting the money in the mailbag, I don't want to lose any of it when we jump. I'll arrange things round here that oughta take some of the heat off us."

Helman bent down and placed his pistol near Woodrow's right hand. Then, taking a pistol off one of the dead guards he fired a single shot from it through the open door and dropped it on to the floor. He gave Zeb and Stu another humourless grin. "Now it looks like the old man was a real bad-ass killer who took on more guns than he could handle."

"Perole's fire comin' up!" Zeb called out.

Helman slung the mailbag over his shoulder. "OK boys, let's go. It's a long tricky haul back to the States so don't break any bones landin' because I ain't holdin' back for anyone."

Woodrow came to with the wind from the open door blowing freezing cold on him. He struggled up on to

13

his hands and knees, the blood from his wound dripping on to the planking of the car. He had to stay in that position for a minute or two for the bout of stomach-heaving dizziness to pass. Then he saw the dead men and the memory of what had happened came flooding back, clearing his head like a douche of cold water. He noticed the pistol by his hand and the other gun by one of the guard's bodies. He didn't have to check the loads in the pistol, the scenario was clear enough. The son-of-a-bitch, Helman, had set him up. Helman had departed with the money and had left him for dead, to be the fall guy for the killing of the guards. The anger welled up inside Woodrow, temporarily blotting out the pain from his wound. Fortunately Helman had only creased him but he was still as good as dead by being strung up in a few weeks' time for robbery and murder, unless he got the hell out of the baggage car before the chief conductor came along the train to pass a few words, or play a hand of poker with the guards.

Not without some effort and more blinding flashes of pain that nearly sent him prone again, Woodrow got shakily to his feet. He pushed the pistol out into the snow-lined track then with one hand pressed against the side of the car to steady him, slowly, head still pounding painfully, he made his tortuous way to the door. Only the grim, cold determination that somehow he had to get out of this hole Helman and his buddies had dropped him in so that he could track the double-crossing sons-of-bitches down and kill them kept him upright and moving.

Woodrow hesitated a few seconds before clearing the gap separating the cars, thinking of his gruesome fate if he slipped down between the cars. He'd missed death by a bullet by the narrowest of margins, he was now trying to escape a hanging. Would he end up as a bloody smear along

15

several yards of railroad track? To do to himself what Helman had failed to do? So be it, he thought, if that's the way it was written out for him in the Book of Life. But he sure as hell wouldn't find what fate had in store for him standing here worrying like some old woman. Woodrow gritted his teeth, let go the handrail, and stepped over the frightening gap. And that was as far as he could consciously remember going. On stepping safely on to the opposite platform he passed out again. He fell against the door with such force that it burst open and he landed in the aisle with a suddenness that raised frightened cries from the female passengers.

When he opened his eyes again Woodrow found himself lying full-length on his seat and felt the tightness of some sort of a bandage around his brow. His head was still throbbing with pain and he realized the train had stopped. The two ladies who had been his travelling companions were

16

sitting on their seats looking at him with anxious-eyed gazes. "He's coming round, Officer," he heard one of them say. Mabel, if he remembered her name correctly.

A big, burly man, wearing the uniform of the Royal Canadian Mounted Police with three gold chevrons on his right arm stepped into his view. Woodrow felt a wave of panic sweep over him and he tried to lever himself upright.

"You just lie back and take it easy, mister . . . " the sergeant said, pushing him gently back on to the seat.

Woodrow told the sergeant his latest alias. "Jackson, Wilber Jackson, Sergeant."

"Well you've had a lucky escape, Mr Jackson", the mountie continued. "The sonsuvbitches . . . " The sergeant cast an apologetic glance at the two matrons. "Beggin' your pardon, ladies," he said, then he switched his hard-faced attention on to Woodrow again. "The men who shot you, Mr Jackson, killed three guards and stole a big payroll. We know that there's at least four in the gang, the three who followed you out of the car and did the killing and robbery and one, m'be two, waiting with the horses at the head of the pass."

"I couldn't rightly tell you how many of them there were, Sergeant," Woodrow smoothly lied. "It all happened so quick. I'd just stepped outside to enjoy a cigar when someone pistol-whipped me. I don't know how long I was out but when I was struggling to get back on to my feet again, wonderin' what the hell was goin' on, one of the bastards fired at me from the doorway of the baggage car." Woodrow shot the ladies a forgive-me-look for the use of the barroom language. The mountie sergeant nodded thoughtfully, accepting Woodrow's account of the way things had happened. "It figures that they didn't want to raise the alarm by firing a pistol just outside this car but when they saw that they hadn't laid you out for a long spell they couldn't afford not to gun you down. I reckon

18

by then they were ready to jump off the train. I've sent my two constables back along the track to where they left the train to pick up their trail from there. They must be well on their way to Montana by now." The sergeant favoured Woodrow with a grimace of a smile. "I opine that they're countrymen of yours, Mr Jackson. I'll send a wire to the law officer at Fort Benton putting him in the picture so that he can try to cut their sign on his side of the line."

Woodrow cursed. He had spent almost nine months setting up the raid, his last year in the Pen planning it all out in his head. He had rented himself a room from a widow woman in Cross Creeks, Montana, a small town north of Bear Paw mountain, within spitting distance of the Canadian line, putting it around that he was a New York real estate agent who had come north on his doctor's advice to get some healthy mountain air inside him, his prison pallor accenting his supposed chest complaint. His regular two or three-day trips into the high country, living like a mountain man, were the building up of his cover for when he made the longer trip into Canada for the actual raid.

Helman and his boys were holed-up in a panhandler's derelict shack on the lower slopes of Bear Paw mountain under strict orders to keep out of Cross Creeks. After the raid, when Helman and his crew had gone their separate ways, he intended staying on in Cross Creeks for a day or two before announcing that his health had improved so much that he was returning to New York. When the lawmen got round to checking out Cross Creeks for strangers seen in the district, men who could have been the train robbers, an elderly gentleman from New York who had been staying in town almost nine months wouldn't fit into the category of a suspicious stranger. Now the situation was all changed. As he had told Helman, any killing would set off a real wide-loop search, and a fast one.

Lawmen could ride into Cross Creeks before he had gathered up his gear and departed. Though he had been out of circulation for more than sixteen years there could still be badge-toting men who knew who he was if they met face to face. Which wouldn't be surprising, Woodrow modestly thought. He had, in his heyday, after the James and the Youngers, been the most sought after outlaw in the south-west, with his likeness pinned up in marshals' offices and barn doors throughout three States.

Helman had sure lit a fire under his ass. He had to rib-kick it to places well away from Montana, but fast, before the flames consumed him whole, some spot where he could get himself organized and set up a hunt of his own. In all the years of his raiding Woodrow had never killed anyone. M'be winged a few lawmen hanging too close to his tail, but now he had a real mean killing streak in his soul. One that wouldn't burn out till Helman and his boys paid in full for their double-cross and the longer he stayed on the train the colder their trail would be.

"The good ladies have cleaned up your wound the best they could," he heard the mountie say, "but my advice is to let a doctor have a look at it when you get to wherever you're bound for. I would take it real easy till then."

"Why, that was right Christian-minded of you ladies," Woodrow said with real feeling. "And I will take it steady so that your good work won't be wasted." Which was, he thought, the second lie he had told the ladies. That upset him somehow. Had he, after a lifetime of thieving, suddenly developed a conscience? If he had he reckoned he was too late for redemption. He had been destined for a place in front of the fiery furnaces of hell a long, long time ago.

The train gave a shuddering series of jerks as it began to slowly pull away. "It's time I was leaving, Mr

Jackson," the mountie said, "and see what progress my men have made. Don't forget about what I said about having that wound seen to. You're not a youngster any more, able to shake a thing like that off in an hour or two." He raised his hat in greeting to the ladies then hurried along the car to drop off before the train built up speed.

Woodrow smiled wanly at the two ladies and lay back and closed his eyes. As much as he craved for the healing rest of a good sleep, that was a medicine he couldn't afford to take. The hangman's noose was swinging too close to him to fret over a bullet crease on the head, however painful it was. Regina was the next stop along the track and whatever physical state he was in he had to leave the train there. His put-by cash was in his room, money he may need in an emergency. And he was in one hell of a tight corner now.

He had enough money on him to

hire a horse to get him to Cross Creeks, but a man who could be possibly travelling one jump ahead of a marshal's posse had no time to stop on the trail to earn money to pay for his and his horse's needs. The conductor coming into the car and calling out, "We're pullin' into Regina in five minutes, folks," brought Woodrow sitting up, eyes open. He swung his feet on to the floor. "I think I'll take a stroll outside when the train pulls in at the depot," he told the ladies. "The fresh air might clear my head."

With disapproving glances from the ladies Woodrow got to his feet. Slipping his heavy ankle-length waterproof over his shoulders, he made his way to the door, trying hard not to let the pain he was suffering with every step he took from showing in his face. If it was almost killing him walking the few paces to the door, he thought, what would it be like sitting up on a horse? And again the picture of Helman in front of his gunsights gave him the grit to keep going.

★ ★ ★

Helman and his boys crossed the Montana line whooping and laughing like a bunch of trail-hands sighting the whorehouses and gin palaces of Wichita after a six-week cattle drive from below the Red. They had pushed their horses down from the high country at a killing pace knowing that just across the border were fresh horses waiting for them in a makeshift corral, enabling them to keep up their headlong dash before marshals' posses cut off the main trails leading out of the border regions. Half an hour later they were jubilantly throwing saddles and gear on to remounts. Then it was time to divvy up the raid takings.

"Boys," said Helman, "I oughta have left some of this in the old fart's pocket so that he could get decently planted. He sure knew his business. Without his plannin' we would have run our mounts into the ground like a bunch of bare-assed Apache and ended up on foot, easy meat for any posse." He mounted up. "Now let's head south and put all this money to good use."

Stu grinned. "I know what I'm spendin' my cut on. I ain't had a good lay for weeks. And that's all I've been thinkin' about sittin' in that ball-freezin' shack."

2

WHEN Helman and his boys made Rapid City, South Dakota, they sold their horses and gear and got themselves rigged out in store-bought suits and continued their travelling south by railroad. A cursory glance by any lawmen, not noticing the bulge of a holstered pistol each had beneath his jacket would tag the four as city dudes, drummers, real-estate men, heading south to separate the back-country folk from their hard-earned dollars.

Helman wasn't travelling south by railroad just to put as much territory between him and the hell the raid would have raised behind him. He had already planned what he was going to do with his share of the takings from the heist. He intended moving in the cattle-dealing trade in a big way. That meant operating below the Red, in Texas and New Mexico. There was a lot of money to be made in the beef market. A longhorn eating its heart out on the western plains was only worth a few dollars. Its price rose five or six times in the Kansas stockyards.

The profit margins rose a lot higher if the buying price was lower. Like, if the beef was stolen and the men who did the stealing wanted quick, cash-on-the-barrel head, deals. And the men who were doing the buying weren't fussy about bills of sale. He had talked over his scheme with Perole before the raid and he had been all for it. The 'breed's connections below the Rio Grande could enable him to get his hands on a regular supply of stolen *gringo* cattle at knockdown prices. He would need a ranch, or some such holding place near the Mex border, extra men, even if Zeb and Stu wanted in, to handle the cattle this side of the Rio Grande. Zeb and Stu had to be in on the deal. He needed their money to fund the operation till the expected high yield returns came rolling in. He had toyed with the idea of arranging Zeb and Stu's sudden demise, the way he had with the old man and take their share. But Zeb and Stu were wide-awake *hombres*, slept on their bellies with pistols in their hands. It would be, he thought, a real darn shame if the boys just blew all that money on liquor and cathouse whores. He would have to try to sweet-talk them into joining him and Perole in the deal.

An hour or so before the train pulled into the depot at Kansas City, being that his end of the car was empty of any other passengers, he put his scheme to Zeb and Stu, and the necessity of giving him some of their cash. Shut-faced the pair listened to his sales talk.

"Why, don't you see, boys," he pleaded, "in two or three years time we'll be bigger cattle-dealers than old John S. Chisum of the Jingle Bob outfit way down in New Mexico territory.

Then you can buy a whole cathouse for yourselves, a saloon, why, a whole goddamned town, if you want, all legal-like, live like real honest citizens."

Stu looked at Zeb before saying his piece. "I dunno, Helman," he said, "me and Zeb were really set to paint Kansas City red. You know, heavy drinkin', gamblin'." He grinned at Zeb. "We've got a bet goin' between us, just who can lay the most women in a night."

Helman smiled, outwardly. Inside he was thinking that the two assholes carried what little brains they had in their pants.

"Why there ain't no need for you boys to miss out on your pleasures. Spend a couple weeks here. Me and Jose will push on into the Nations, get us some extra hands for all the beef we're goin' to buy." His face and eyes hardened. "Remember boys, don't forget you've got to meet me and Jose's contribution if you want in."

"We'll pay our dues when the time

comes, Helman," Zeb promised. "After we've had our fun. Won't we, Stu?"

"You can bet on it, Helman," said Stu.

"I hope so," replied Helman. "Or you're both out of the deal. Savvy *compadres*? If everything goes as planned me and Perole should be back in Kansas City to pick up you boys in, as I say, about a couple weeks." He gave another one of his frosty-eyed grins. "And try not to burn the town down before I ride back."

3

BIG SAM BIGELOW, owner of the Silver Dollar, stood at the head of the broad, red-carpeted stairs that led to the private rooms. He chewed contentedly at the end of his cigar as he listened to the sweet music of the cash registers tinging away, nonstop, at the shoulder-to-shoulder crowded bar. The gambling tables were also coining in the cash. And so they should be, Big Sam thought, the Silver Dollar was the best run saloon in Kansas City.

The four big men, wide shoulders straining at the seams of their black, formal evening-wear jackets, positioned at strategic points around the saloon were there to keep it the best run saloon in town. Any sudden flare up of trouble or rowdiness they would stomp on it before it could cause any annoyance to the rest of the saloon's clientele. Big Sam cast a sweeping gaze on the eight girls, whose dresses exposed black fishnet-stocking-clad legs three inches above their knees, weaving their way through the press at the gambling tables. Pausing to pass the time of day with this one, smilingly commiserating at another one on hearing of his bad luck, they were equally adept, in their own suggestive-voiced, sweet-smiling way, as his hard-faced bouncers in keeping the lid on things. Big Sam didn't rue them one cent of their pay.

Zeb and Stu pushed open the double glass doors of the Silver Dollar then paused in their strides, gazing open-mouthed at the long redwood bar, the glistening chandeliers, and the girls. "Whoee Zeb," Stu mouthed. "There ain't nothin' like this in Ozark County. Look at them whatsits on that blonde at the roulette tables. Ain't they something?"

Zeb nodded non-committally. Wanted

by the law in several States self-preservation came before eyeing bosoms, however tantalizingly big. Thoroughly he took in the whole saloon, rear entrances if needed, and easily picked out the bouncers. He couldn't see the shotguns he knew they would have close at hand.

"Stu," he said, as they walked over to the bar, "have your fun but don't forget you ain't in Ozark County and nights out don't have to end in rib-kickin' and knifin'. So take it easy on the liquor. There's six hardcases scattered about the place, big enough to contain a full-scale riot. Any trouble and we'll be out in the street on our ears, or behind bars in the local jail. And the sheriff will get to wonderin' where we've got all this foldin' money we've got stitched in belts wrapped around our bellies. If he figures it out he'll call in the state marshals and we'll be sailing up Shit Creek. And Mr Helman won't like that at all."

Grinning, Stu said, "We coulda left

our pokes in the hotel safe, Zeb."

Zeb gave him a withering glance. "With all these safe-robbers about?"

* * *

A sour-faced Stu had watched his several hundred dollars of winnings being raked off the board by the roulette croupier, now he was seeing his stake money going the same way. Gloria, the big-breasted blonde Stu had first seen on entering the saloon snuggled closer into his side, giving him the full treatment of the warm softness of her best feature. "You keep betting, honey," she said, her smile all blue-eyed innocence. "Your luck is bound to ride high again."

Gloria knew for certain that even if the Angel Gabriel was hovering over the hick she was conning to keep on gambling his luck wouldn't change. Big Sam's croupier would see to that, then she would get her bonus for keeping a sucker throwing his money away till he was flat broke.

Zeb, not gambling himself, said, "Call it a night, Stu. You ain't goin' to beat the house, not with shit's own luck you're carryin'."

Stu ignored his advice. Grinning drunkenly at Gloria he placed all his chips on black seven. Zeb cursed under his breath. The way the big-breasted bitch was rubbing herself against Stu the horn dog wouldn't leave the table till he had lost all his cut from the robbery. Stu had hard-assed all the way to Canada, risked his neck in the heist for damn all.

The croupier, a small, thin-faced, fancy frilled-shirt-garbed man called, "All bets placed, gents?" and put out a hand to spin the wheel.

Zeb favoured him with a long, searching look. A natural-born suspicious man he smelt a rat. He firmly believed that most men, given the opportunity, with no risk attached, would steal to increase their finances. The railroad barons stole land from the sodbusters to lay their tracks; the whites were stealing everything the Indians thought was theirs; the big real-estate men were foreclosing land tenancy rights on ragged-assed sharecroppers, all legal and above board. There were more heisters roaming around the territory than those like him and Stu who wore masks and carried pistols.

Zeb had no doubt that the big, lard-gutted, cigar-smoking bastard, he reckoned was the owner of the saloon, was pulling in a few extra bucks by running a fixed roulette wheel. Zeb kept his gaze fixed on the weasel-faced croupier.

After he had spun the wheel the croupier placed his hands on the edge of the table, fingers splayed, leaning slightly forward watching the run of the ball. As the wheel began to slow down Zeb saw the croupier straighten up and his right hand slowly slipping out of sight over the edge of the table. Zeb's face boned over. You tinhorn son-of-a-bitch, he thought. He pulled out his pistol, drew back the hammer and pointed it at the croupier's head.

"Keep both hands in view," he grated, "or I'll blow your head clear off your shoulders. This asshole, folks, is riggin' the wheel." The players at the table drew back sharply from Zeb as though he was a plague carrier. "Look at the cheatin' sonuvabitch's face, Stu. Don't you see that the game's crooked? There'll be some sorta switch under the table to alter the run of the ball. And that big-breasted bitch snuckin' up to you is part of the setup."

The little croupier stood, hands outstretched on the table, unmoving as though frozen in time, his face a blood-drained mask of fear as he eyeballed the big Colt held steady on him.

Zeb raised his voice, silencing, stilling all noise and movement in the saloon. "You, mister, up there on the balcony, I reckon you're the bossman, me and my pard don't want any trouble so hold off your strongarm boys! We'll take what we think this tinhorn owes us then we'll leave all quiet and peaceful-like. Make a move against us and we'll shoot our way out. And that will kinda make a mess of this grand place you're runnin'. Is it a deal, mister? Do we play it cool?"

And that was the way Zeb wanted it, cool. Close contact with the law if any shooting took place, even if in self-defence, wasn't something he desired. One question could lead to another, then another, and Stu being drunk wasn't up to being questioned. He could say the wrong thing then the Western Union telegraph wires between Kansas City and Canada could be humming and within the week a hanging judge could be riding into town.

Stu thought otherwise. Inflamed by the amount of liquor he had downed, and led to a fleecing like some greenhorn kid by a whore touched him on several raw-nerve ends. Mad-crazy he turned and dealt the blonde a heavy

39

backhanded swipe across the face that sent her sprawling across the roulette table, scattering the chips. The blood streaming from her lacerated gums darkened the covering of the table.

Stu swung around and faced the roulette croupier and with face working in anger he yanked out his pistol and pumped two shells into the little man's chest. The croupier's fancy white shirt blossomed two rapidly spreading red patches and he spun away from the table as though jerked back by an invisible wire. Then, losing his balance, he fell straight and true, like a felled tree, to the ground.

"You mad-assed bastard, Stu!" Zeb cried. "You're goin' to get us into a real shootin' match!"

For several seconds they stood there, grimfaced, pistols swinging in a slow arc, covering as much of the saloon floor as they could, trying to keep command of the situation. The calm broke when one of the bouncers brought up his shotgun waist high.

Before he could fire it Zeb picked him off with a single head shot. The bouncer rocked back on his heels then, folding at the middle, fell down heavily, his dying reflexes pulling at the triggers of the shotgun, the double loads blasting a chandelier into a thousand pieces. The showering glass shards broke the customers' rigid stances, sent them yelling and screaming heading for the door or diving for shelter under tables.

"Down the bastards!" Big Sam screeched. "Before they wreck the place!"

Stu triggered off a shot at him. Cursing and crying with pain Big Sam staggered back several paces, clutching at his shattered left elbow.

Another bouncer attempted to earn his due the hard way. He leapt up from behind an upturned table and fired at Zeb, the pistol's shell whizzing close by Zeb's ear. Zeb and Stu fired at him together and the bouncer flopped back down behind the table, his trouble-shooting for Big Sam ended forever.

"Let's get to hell outa here, Stu," Zeb said. "We won't get the chance to reload and the law could come fire-ballin' in at anytime."

Slowly they sidled towards the door, tensed up as hound dogs in heat, the proven deadly accuracy of their shooting giving them a knife's blade thin edge. They missed seeing a barkeep laying a long-barrelled shotgun on them from across the bar top. The noise of the double barrels being pulled off rattled the chandeliers, causing more panic to the bellies-to-the-floor customers.

The left-hand side of Stu's face and neck catching most of the shotgun's blast was stripped to the bone in a fearful welter of blood and shredded flesh, killing him instantaneously. He fell away from Zeb and their slight edge had gone.

A fusillade of pistol shots struck Zeb. Wolf-snarling in pain he shook his head like a wounded buffalo trying to clear the red haziness that was rapidly obscuring his vision. He tried to swing his pistol round to fire back at his assailants and found that he couldn't make his limbs respond, it was as though his body no longer belonged to him. He dirty-mouthed himself for being so weak as he slowly sank to his knees alongside Stu. More shells hit him but he was beyond feeling any pain. His last fleeting, lucid thought as the total darkness of death overwhelmed him was that they had sure whooped it up in Kansas City.

Big Sam came down the stairs, face white and drawn with pain, angrily eyeing the mayhem. "The trouble's all over folks!" he called out. "Drinks on the house, gents. Just step up to the bar and name your fancy. And get the music goin'!" He walked across to the bouncers, pistols still drawn, standing over the bodies of Zeb and Stu. Beady-eyeing them he snapped, "Dead, I hope!" Getting an affirmative nod back from one of the bouncers he added, "Well don't just stand there gazin' at them! Get them and the other bodies carried out back then get the place straightened up. And get me the doc, *pronto*. I'll be in my office. Bring Gloria in, then he can see us both."

Big Sam sat at his desk nursing his wounded arm, the low, painful moaning of the semiconscious Gloria lying on the settee making him as irritable as his own wound was. He heard a knock on the door and barked, "Come in!" One of the bouncers came into the office. Scowling with pain Big Sam snarled, "Where the hell's the doc? Stuck in some poker game?"

"He's on his way, boss," replied the bouncer. "But I thought you'd like to see these before he came." He laid two well-filled money-belts on the desk, one with ominous dark, still damp stains on it. He opened the bloodstained belt, showing Big Sam the edges of the wads of dollar bills. "We took them off the two wild-asses, boss."

Big Sam forgot his pain for a minute

or two while he rapidly calculated how much money the belts held. "Jesus!" he exclaimed. "They must have been carrying the contents of a town's bank around with them. Who the hell are they?"

The bouncer shrugged his shoulders. "Dunno, boss. The James and the Younger boys are either dead or behind bars. And I ain't heard of any other gang that's carryin' on where they left off."

Big Sam managed to give a grimace of a smile. "It's an ill-wind that don't do some good to some *hombre*. They sure won't need it where they're restin' now, that's for sure, so I reckon that findies bein' keepies, the cash is mine. It'll pay for the damage the bastards have caused." Then feeling an extra spasm of pain and hearing Gloria beginning to sob as she came to, he said angrily, "Go and ass-kick the doc if you have to, to get the sonuvabitch here!"

4

BLUE DUCK had never seen the two men, a hatchet-faced white and a Mexican breed, in Carr's Whiskey Palace before. Shorty Carr's grandly named 'Palace' was a ramshackle barn of a dump, part bar, part sutler's stores, set alongside where the Turtle Creek trail cut the Harrison Plank road.

Though the whiskey Shorty Carr sold was judged by hard-liquor men as pure bull's piss, unfit for even the most firewater-craving Indian to drink, the Palace saw a regular to and fro of customers. The Palace played a key role in the way some types of businesses were run in the Nations.

It was a place where deals were struck, where men sought like-minded men to carry out a bank raid, a stagecoach hold-up, cattle-lifting, or a plain out and out bushwhacking to even up a wrong done. A place where walls didn't have ears, Shorty Carr being diplomatically blind and deaf. And his three hired hands, Indian 'breed whiskey soaks, didn't give a hoot what the white eyes were discussing, even if they knew enough of the white eyes' tongue to savvy what they were talking about.

Blue Duck saw Shorty Carr's moon-like face widen in a smile of welcome as the 'breed came up to the bar so the very slight probability that the two strangers could be drifters, passing through the Nations seeking work at some Texas ranch was wrong thinking on his part. They had pulled in at Shorty's for business reasons, unlawful business. In no time at all the three were close-talking, the white man doing most of it. Occasionally Shorty would nod his head as if agreeing with something the white man had said. He was shifty-assed, curious to know the nature of the business being talked

47

over. M'be he could get a piece of the action? But it was a decidedly unhealthy pastime in the Nations to start asking strangers questions before being invited to say your piece.

"Who's that ferret-faced kid?" Helman asked Shorty. "If his ears flap any harder he'll fly over here. He's askin' to get plugged."

Shorty laughed. "Don't worry about him, Mr Helman, that's Blue Duck. Puts it about that he's part Cherokee, but he's as white as you or me. He also puts it about that he once rode with the Younger boys, but that's likewise bullshit. Him and another two drifters tried their hand at cattle-liftin' once, got stomped on hard by the law. The kid would have swung alongside his two buddies if Belle Starr, who kinda has the hots for him, hadn't spent a heap of money bailin' him out."

"That little runt's shacked up with Belle?" Perole said in disbelief. "Some come down from being bounced by Cole Younger. She must have gone soft in her old age."

"I don't know about that, Jose," Shorty replied. "I hear she's still ornery as ever. Still thinks that she's Queen of Younger's Bend."

"Would he be useful as one of the men I need?" Helman asked.

"Nah," said Shorty. "Belle would slice the kid's balls off if he took up with any enterprise without her sayso. And you don't want Belle to know your business, Mr Helman. When she's drunk they'll hear her blabbing clear all the way to Fort Smith. As I told you, I'll get the word out and in five, six days from now I'll have a dozen good cattle-moving men sitting here waiting for you." He grinned at Helman. "They won't be fussy whose cattle they're gonna move as long as the payment's right."

"You do that, Mr Carr," said Helman. "But don't spread it all over the territory I'm wantin' men. Belle Starr won't be the only one in the Nations with a loud mouth."

e accompanying snake-eyed look nan gave him and the frightening understanding that Helman would hold him responsible if the news of Helman's hiring men became widespread, gave Shorty an inner chill. If that happened it was not beyond reasonable thinking that Shorty's Whiskey Palace would require a new owner. Not trusting himself to speak Shorty gave a wide-nodding, trust-me grin.

"Good," said Helman. "You'll get your due when I'm satisfied with the men you bring in, OK?"

It wasn't OK. But Shorty wasn't going to tell that to Helman's face, not without a shotgun, hammers back, in his hands. He just gave another ass-kissing smile.

Helman picked up a bottle of whiskey and two glasses and walked over to the only other table in the place and sat down. Perole, after a few parting words with Shorty joined him. Helman poured out the drinks.

"You ride south, Jose," Helman said.

"Find a quiet spot where cattle can be bedded down. You know what's needed, plenty of water and good grass, and well away from a regular cattle trail. I'll go and pick up Zeb and Stu; I'll probably have to lift them up on to their saddles. I'll meet up with you here. By then that fat greaseball should have the men we need. Then we'll all ride south and start up our cattle-dealing business."

Blue Duck noted that they only downed two whiskies then left which got him thinking that whatever business they had set up with Shorty it was rolling along at high speed. Shorty walked out back and it was only a matter of minutes before Blue Duck saw two of Shorty's hired hands ride out at speed. Whatever caper the two strangers were organizing, he thought, it had definitely got Shorty moving fast as well. He got to his feet when Shorty returned inside and strode over to the bar. He knew the strangers' names, Jose and Helman, Helman he reckoned, being the bossman. He began to pump Shorty about the nature of their business with him.

Shorty scowled. "Now you know I can't tell you that, Blue Duck. I'm trusted in the whole territory as an hombre with tight-buttoned-up lips. All I can tell you is that Mr Helman wants to hire a bunch of men who can handle cattle. Whose cattle, well, your guess is as good as mine as I ain't privy to Mr Helman's plans. But I opine that it will be a big operation, well outa your league, Blue Duck. And Mr Helman looks a mean sonuvabitch to work for." Shorty Carr grinned. "You stay at Younger's Bend, Blue Duck, and keep Belle Starr warm in bed."

Blue Duck knew what Shorty had told him was right. He was never more than a penny-ante cattle thief but he sure didn't want to spend the rest of his natural at Younger's Bend, humping a woman old enough to be his ma whenever she got the urge. He walked back to the table and finished his drink then left to ride back to Younger's Bend, promising himself that he would try to make it his business to be in Shorty's Palace when the men Shorty had sent out for showed up, hoping that Mr Helman would hire him along with the rest of the hardcases.

5

WOODROW LIDDELL, alias the self-ordained Reverend Joshua Simms, gave the burly, florid-faced, cigar-smoking man sitting opposite him a preacher's soft-smiling admonishing look. Unmoved by the silent plea that he was causing discomfort to the female passengers in the south-bound stage from Wichita, Kansas to Fort Reno in the Indian Territory, the big man favoured Woodrow with a stompin'-man's kiss-my-ass scowl and continued filling the coach with the acrid smoke of a cheap cigar.

Woodrow, not wanting to blow his latest cover, clutched the Bible resting on his knees tighter. Resisting the temptation to reach across and ram the roll of horse droppings the son-of-a-bitch thought was a cigar down his throat, reluctantly he let the matter drop. He had more pressing things on his mind, such as the whereabouts of Helman and his boys, and that the elderly invalid who had stayed a spell at Cross Creeks, Montana, had, as far as the law was concerned, vanished from the face of the earth. But he did comfort himself with the pleasant thought that if he ever ran into the big man again, and opportunity presented itself, he would lay the Colt he carried, most un-preacher-like under his left arm, against his head.

Woodrow had travelled down from Montana by river boat, disembarking at Independence, Missouri, then by rail to Wichita, Kansas. The slower boat journey gave him the time to recuperate from his near miss with death. How he had managed to sit up on his horse on the ride from Regina, where he had bought a mount and rations for the trip to Cross Creeks, had Woodrow beat. By nature and profession he wasn't a religious man but he thought that some fate, or Great Spirit, as the Indians believed in, who had got him safely across the gap between the railcars, had been alongside him on the ride. Kept him from falling off his horse to end up come the thaw just a heap of bones on the trail, so that he continued on his vengeance trail.

If that was so, Woodrow thought hopefully, it would be only a matter of time before he met up with the double-crossing sons-of-bitches. And then, as sure as the hell he was bound for in the afterlife, he would make that hope turn into grim reality by gunning them down. He had no direct lead to where Helman could be, other than a gut feeling that he would be running around in the last stomping grounds of the owlhoots, the Nations, Indian Territory.

In the short time he had known Helman, he hadn't talked like the rest of his boys, of the whoring and drinking they would indulge in with their cut of the raid. He catalogued him as a penny-ante thief wanting to make it to the big time. To live in a fine-built house, mix with the big political wheels in the territory. He had taken the first step on that road by grabbing more than his share of the loot.

In the Nations, the hold-outs' territory, he would feel safe from any threat from Montana lawmen, or any state law. West of the Pecos the only law was thinly administered by hard-pressed marshals working out of Fort Smith, Arkansas, for Judge Parker serving papers on specific named owlhoots. It was a big country and Woodrow knew he would need a lot of luck to cut Helman's sign. News of his whereabouts would be gleaned from saloons and bawdy-houses, establishments so brimful of sin that a preacher couldn't be seen even lying dead in them. Eyebrows would be raised in surprise and wonder and publicity was something he needed like another bullet furrow in the head. Woodrow leaned back against his seat and closed his eyes, all this thinking was giving him a bad head; he had done enough of it for one day. He would meet that problem when he came to it.

* * *

Cal Lewis saw the dust haze moving up the grade and took a final swig of Jim Crow then threw the bottle away. He mounted his horse and tied a dun-coloured bandana round the lower part of his face, thinking that though the whiskey had fired his blood somewhat it had done damn all to steady his nerves for the task ahead. He still felt an urgent need to pay a visit to the crapper rather than ride out of the brush and hold up a stage.

The only robbing he had done had been as a kid, stealing apples from a barrel on the town's general store's porch. It was a big, unknown and dangerous step he was about to take, heisting a stage. Cal wasn't intent on taking up being a road agent as a way of regularly earning his keep, he had seen more than a few men who had taken up that trade being hauled off in a marshal's tumbleweed wagon to stand trial in front of 'Hanging' Judge Parker at Fort Smith, Arkansas; some of them all shot to hell who wouldn't make it to Fort Smith, robbing Judge Parker of the pleasure of stringing them up.

All he wanted was a decent grubstake so that he could make the trip to California and make his fortune in the goldfields. A dollar a day and all-found tending longhorns, or working his ass off walking behind an ornery-tempered mule ploughing a barren, stony section of land, weren't chores for a man who wanted to make his way in the world. He was broke to the wide now, at nineteen; he sure didn't want to stay a saddle-bum all his life.

The stage driver yanked at the reins and heeled on the brake as the coach rocked over the last rise, drawing it to a high dust-raising halt. He twisted his ass in his seat and yelled into the coach,

"Ten minutes halt, folks, to give the horses a breather before we roll back down on to the flats!" He grinned at his shotgun guard. "There's plenty of thick brush hereabouts if you want more than just to stretch your legs!"

Woodrow stepped down from the coach first, giving a helping hand to the two ladies to do likewise. They were followed by the big cigar-smoking man and the last passenger, a little, fat, city-dressed man whom Woodrow took to be a drummer. The driver and the guard were already on the ground checking on the horses' straps and reins. Cal kneed his horse out of the brush brandishing a double-barrelled shotgun.

"Don't any of you folks move!" he called out. "And no one need get hurt." He stopped his horse a few feet from the coach and swung down from his saddle. Close-eyeing the guard and driver he said, "You just pull those pistols out, real slow-like, and throw them this way. No tricks or your passengers will get both barrels, and the company won't like to hear how your foolishness got some passengers killed."

Both men gave Cal fish-eyed glares but did as they had been told, the driver saying, "You're wastin' your time, kid, we ain't carryin' a payroll."

"I ain't after gold," Cal replied. "I'll be satisfied to take what these three *hombres* are carrying." His tough, no-nonsense voice belied his nervous fears that things could go wrong. If they did he would cut and run for it. He was in one big hurry to get himself a grubstake but wasn't desperate enough to shed blood to get it.

The gun stuck into the belly of the smallest of the male passengers, the frightened-looking drummer, got Cal a gold watch and chain, and a heavy feeling wallet, giving him the confidence in his ability to get his grubstake with no fuss at all. He reckoned he should have no problem either relieving the tall, horse-faced preacher of any cash he was holding. "Now your wallet, preacher-man," he said, moving closer to him.

Woodrow looked sadly down at him. "Would you rob a man of the cloth, my son?" he said fatherly.

"I ain't about to rob the ladies, Reverend," Cal replied. "And I calculate the driver and the guard are only carrying loose change in their pockets. That only leaves you three gents and the horses. If I don't rob you it's hardly been worth the trouble to come out and rob the stage."

Woodrow knew that the kid was a greenhorn at stage-heisting. Robbing a stage was at least a two-man chore, good men, unless the robber was a cold-blooded killer like Helman and shot dead the guard and driver. That action, killing the only men who had a chance of saving them from being robbed, would scare the passengers into being real co-operative. On his own, without a pard covering him with a rifle from the brush, the kid didn't know that he was as good as dead.

Once the kid had robbed them and ridden off, as soon as they were out of shotgun range the guard, or the driver, would grab for the rifle the kid had failed to see lying on the footrest of the seat. Before the kid reached the covering shelter of the brush his back would be well and truly holed with Winchester shells. Woodrow, once a greenhorn himself, decided to save the kid from an earlier death than he was anticipating, reckoning that a spell in jail, if he still wanted to rob stages he could ponder over what had gone wrong on this one, was a heap less painful and fatal to the constitution than being shot in the back. Still smiling his preacher's sad smile for not persuading an out-and-out sinner to step back on to the straight and narrow, he reached under his coat.

Cal yelped like a kicked dog as the foresight of a Colt pistol was jabbed under his nose. "Now, sinner," Woodrow said, his voice no longer soft, preacher-like. "Have I to upset further these good ladies by seeing your head splattered against the side of the coach? Or are you going to drop that scatter-gun on to the ground?"

Through tear-glazed eyes, head ricked painfully back, Cal peered up at Woodrow, and couldn't see an ounce of Christian charity showing in the hard-angled face. Seemingly on its own accord the shotgun slipped from his hands and fell to the ground. The Indian-face softened slightly.

"A sensible move, sinner," said Woodrow.

In spite of his bulk the cigar-smoking man could move fast. He bent over and picked up the shotgun and with his face working in anger he drove the butt at Cal's face. "Take that you sonuvabitch!" he snarled.

Woodrow's reaction was just that mite faster. His pistol swept down, striking the big man across the fingers of his right hand. He cried out with pain and the shotgun hit the dirt for a second time. Woodrow hard-eyed the big man. "The boy will get his just deserts from a court of law." Then, so that the women could not hear, he said softly, but menacingly, "Not from some big fat asshole who's set himself up as a regulator."

Pain-angry, the big man opened his mouth to protest, loudly and profanely at being pistol-whipped till he saw the black muzzle hole of the Colt now aimed directly at his nose and the preacher's hard, unyielding glare. Suddenly the pain in his hand and his equally hurt pride didn't seem to matter any more. He scowled at Woodrow but ate crow. Spinning round on his heels he clambered back into the coach. Only then did he recollect that he had been called an asshole by a preacher. Strangely he didn't think that was unusually strong language for a preacher to use. Not when he knew for certain that the son-of-a-bitch, preacher-man or not, would have had no hesitation in plugging him if he had pushed it to a showdown.

"I'll take charge of the kid, Reverend," the guard said, retrieving his and the driver's pistols. "He'll be out of your way tied up on top of the coach. And I can keep an eye on him up there. I'll hand him over to the sheriff at Plattesville." He gave Woodrow a quizzical glance. "I ain't seen a preacher pull out a hogleg so fast before." The guard pushed back his hat and scratched vigorously at his scalp. "Come to think of it I've never seen a pistol-totin' sky-pilot before."

Woodrow cold-grinned him back. "I'm not one of your mealy-mouthed preachers, friend, preaching forgiveness to your enemies, give them the other cheek to strike. I preach the Old Testament religion, an eye for an eye and hell and damnation to your enemies. David didn't sweet-talk Goliath, did he, friend? With God's help and a sure-fired stone he laid Goliath low. I've been passing the word of God among the settlers in the northern territories, and as sure as there are fiery furnaces in hell, our heathen red brethren that are abroad in those lands, pay no heed to any sweet-talk. So like Gideon I go girded for war." Woodrow's smile broadened. "I'm too old to wield a sword so I put my trust in the Lord and Mr Samuel Colt."

A dumbfounded guard pulled his hat back on to his head, thinking that the preacher wasn't the craziest *hombre* he had sat shotgun guard over but he would put him up among the top runners. Then again the Nations made everyone a mite loco in the end. He took the strips of rawhide from the driver and began tying up Cal.

"There's hope for you, sinner," Woodrow told Cal. "You look as though you've just started your back-sliding. A spell in a county jail might put you back on the straight and narrow."

Cal, full up with angry disappointment at seeing his grand plan collapsing when it looked like it was going great

67

guns, gave vent to his rage at the object who had been its downfall. Red-faced, he yelled, "You sanctimonious old bastard, you want to be hungry and stony-broke and see how long you stay on the straight and narrow!"

"Mind your manners, kid," the guard snapped, dragging Cal, still loudly protesting to the coach. "You're lucky we ain't bundlin' you up in a tarp sheet."

Woodrow sadly shook his head at the two female passengers as if asking them to appreciate the hard and often thankless task he had fighting the Devil's sinful ways of living that some men in the Territory had taken up. Inwardly he said, when you cool down, kid, you'll realize what the guard told you ain't nothing but the gospel truth.

6

WOODROW intended only staying a couple of days in Plattesville, time enough to see if he had real good fortune by meeting up with Helman or any of his boys; then to buy himself a horse so that he could spread the gospel among the townships further west in the Territory. Leastways that was the story he was telling anyone curious enough to ask him his business. To stay too long in one locality was risking being asked by the churchgoing citizens to preach a sermon at their next Meeting Day. Then he would be shown up for the fake he was.

He was going to take a chance on paying Belle Starr a visit, if she was still above ground, at her place at Younger's Bend. Younger's Bend had been a regular hole-up for owlhoots who were being pressed too hard by Judge Parker's marshals. Belle ran a regular thieves' kitchen. She had both ears to the ground, would know who was in the territory, who had left it in a hurry. He knew Belle from way back. She would give her last cent to help out a friend in need, and give him her favours just as freely.

But Belle had a weakness, to be loose-mouthed somewhat when she was hitting the bottle. Woodrow could imagine her telling whoever she was sharing her bed with, "Guess who paid me a call, why Woodrow Liddell? That old goat who was robbing stages when Jesse James was still wearing short pants. He's calling himself the Reverend Joshua Simms now, dressed all in preacher's black. I reckon the old sonuvabitch has got religion doing that long spell in San Quentin."

He was still weighing up the risks of visiting Belle when he saw the tumbleweed wagon escorted by a second marshal rumbling out of town on its way to Fort Smith and Judge Parker's courthouse. There were only two prisoners in it, one of them the kid who had tried to rob the stage. Woodrow cursed softly. He hadn't expected him to be hauled off to appear in front of a hard-nosed judge like Parker. The kid hadn't really robbed anyone, or done any of the passengers harm. Judge Parker took a strong line against any wrong-doers, hanging them being his speciality. The kid could be heading for a ten-year stretch in the State Pen.

Woodrow could write a book on how things were in the Pen. The kid would wish he had been shot dead. He had got the kid into it, Woodrow thought, it was up to him to get the kid out of it. Woodrow slow-smiled. He wondered what the old hands would have thought, if they had still been around instead of lying under a patch of dirt on some Boot Hill, him reckoning on heisting a tumbleweed wagon. Woodrow's smile faded as slowly as it had appeared as an idea began to take place in his mind. The kid would make an ideal snooper for him. Young, innocent, country-boy looking, in no way would he be thought of as a marshal, or a bounty-hunter. Asking questions about the whereabouts of particular characters in the Nations was an unhealthy business, for the questioner.

Naturally he would have to persuade the kid to help him out. That shouldn't be a problem, the kid would owe him when he sprung him from the tumbleweed wagon.

★ ★ ★

The wagon bounced high over an extra bumpy stretch of the trail throwing a hand-and-foot shackled Cal hard up against his fellow prisoner, a ploughshare-faced Indian. He mumbled an apology and shuffled back along the wagon bed to the furthest corner away from the Indian. He had heard one of the marshals tell the sheriff of

Plattesville that the Indian, an Agency-jumping Apache, was wanted for five counts of murder, and shooting killings. The unblinking, skin-cringing look the red son-of-a-bitch was giving him his murder tally could rise to six before the wagon reached Fort Smith. Cal had never been so low and miserable in his life before. He would have bawled like a scared-to-death girl if it wouldn't have showed the Indian how shit-frightened he was of him.

A sudden crack of a single rifle shot from a rock fall to the left of the trail startled him. The hat of the marshal driving the wagon jumped off his head as though blown away by a gust of wind and Cal threw himself prone on to the floor of the wagon, sickness of fear clawing at the back of his throat. A killing raid by some buddies of the throat-cutting bastard squatting opposite him, he thought bitterly, would be a fitting end to a day he was wishing he had never woken up to see. Trying to heist a stage had definitely not been one of the best ideas he had come up with to raise himself some cash.

He lifted his head in surprise when he heard a voice yell out from the rocks, "I want the kid released! Send him over here, *pronto*! Any tricks and it'll be your head that will catch the next shot!"

Though the threat of being scalped by broncos had been lifted Cal didn't believe in miracles. He couldn't think of anyone in this neck of the territory, or indeed the whole of the United States of America, who would risk his neck throwing down on two marshals to set him free. More than likely, he thought morbidly, the way his luck had been running lately, it would be the big bastard who had tried to beat his head in when the preacher had him by the balls. This time he could be wanting to string him up on the nearest tree, vigilante style.

The marshal who had had his hat removed sat rigid, as though chiselled from stone. Out of the side of his mouth he said, "Do as the bushwhackin' sonuvabitch says, Ben. The dead-eyed Dick has us between a rock and a hard place."

Ben, hands well away from the pistol holstered on his right hip, dismounted and unlocked the wagon's door. Cal, still thinking that he could be jumping from the skittle into the fire, hesitated before getting to his feet.

"Come on kid! I ain't got all day, shift your ass!" he heard the unknown rifleman shout. "And get your irons off! You stay put, Injun, it ain't Jubilation Day!"

Cal stood up and after the marshal had unlocked his chains he briefly rubbed his ankles and wrists where the irons had rubbed the skin raw before he jumped out of the wagon and ran to the rocks, and his saviour, or so he hoped.

Cal was expected to be surprised by whoever it was who had gone out of his way to rescue him; it was a real big, slackjawed, pop-eyed one when he saw the preacher crouching behind a boulder with a rifle in his hand.

"Jesus God!" he breathed. "You!"

Woodrow greeted him with a beaming smile. "Welcome, sinner. There's horses back there." Woodrow pointed over his shoulder to a small stand of cottonwoods. "Wait there till I see those two *hombres* on their way to Fort Smith." The smile faded and Cal saw the iron-faced look he had been treated to at the stage. "Don't take it in your young head to go harin' off to parts unknown or I'll track you down and take you to Fort Smith myself, alive or dead." The smile returned. "You don't know it yet but I'm bankin' on you and me being pards. I ain't just rescued you out of the goodness of my heart."

"You can mount up and start rollin' the wagon again!" Woodrow shouted. "But, you on the horse, don't take it into your head to swing back this way to try and injun-up on me because I'm layin' down this repeater and pickin'

76

up a Sharps big fifty. From where I'm perchin' this cannon can put a slug right through Judge Parker's front porch door. So if I even see so much as a whiff of your dust headin' this way I'll blow you clear out of the Nations."

"Why you're lyin'!" Cal said, still unable to take in the unusual action of a preacher holding up a tumbleweed wagon. "You ain't got a buffalo gun!"

Woodrow gave him a cold, toothy grin. "It ain't really a black-hearted, wicked lie, kid. And it's for a good cause, saving you from a stretch in the Pen, and durn less sinful than actually putting a slug in that marshal's hide. Because that's what I would have to do if he rides back this way. Now you get over to the horses, I'll watch that pair till it looks as though they're doin' what I told them to do. Then you and me can have a heart-to-heart palaver."

Cal gave Woodrow a narrow-eyed, calculating look. "You sonuvabitch!" he burst out. "You ain't no more of a preacher than I am!"

77

Woodrow's face hardened. "That I ain't, kid, that I ain't. So now you know I'll shoot you down like a mangy dog if you take off before we've had our chat."

"I'm on my way, mister," Cal said, and ran to the trees, stoically thinking of what next life had in store for him, praying that it would be more easier on his nerves than fate had dished out to him the last few days.

* * *

The pair of them had ridden twenty miles west from where Woodrow had held up the marshals' wagon and made camp on the banks of a small stream. While the water for the coffee was coming to the boil Woodrow told Cal why he had saved him from going to jail.

"Like you kid," he began, "I was a stage heister, robbed my first stage when your pa was still in short pants. Done a heap of robbin' since. Did time in the Pen for it." Then he told Cal of being double-crossed by his gang, showing Cal the bullet furrow on his brow as he spoke. He didn't tell him about the killing of the guards and it being a train they had raided. "The sonsuvbitches took all the haul and left me for dead." He thin-grinned. "I'm tryin' to track them down to put things right but I've got to watch my back-trail in case the law jumps me. That's why I'm dressed as a preacher. Though that kinda restricts my snoopin' around in places the bastards who shot me frequent. I'd like you to be my eyes and ears. I'll pay you well, feed you and you'll sleep between sheets in a real bed when we're not on the trail. Is it a deal? It's a lot easier on the constitution than tryin' to rob stages. If it ain't, you're welcome to take the horse and ride to wherever you want to go with no hard feelin's on my side."

In Cal's opinion the big man was crazy trying to seek out men who could be anywhere between the Rio

Grande and the Pacific Ocean though that didn't prevent him coming to a positive decision. Not because he felt that the big man would shoot him dead if he refused his offer in spite of telling him otherwise, but without a horse, food and money Cal knew that he would soon be getting his innards bounced about in the back of a tumbleweed wagon again, if the state marshals didn't kill him first. He stretched out his hand. "It's a deal, Mister er . . . what the heck do I call you?"

Smiling, Woodrow took it in a firm, pard's handshake. "The Reverend Joshua Simms will do for now, and your handle, Kid?"

"Cal, Cal Lewis, Reverend," replied Cal.

"Well Cal," Woodrow said, "we'll get you a new rigout the first town we hit. Do you tote a gun?"

"No I don't," said Cal. He gave Woodrow a kicked-hound's hurt look. "I had a shotgun once. I hope what you're payin' me to do don't mean that I might have to use a six-shooter to get myself out of a hairy situation."

Woodrow favoured Cal with a fatherly smile. "I'm not after hiring myself a *pistolero*. I don't want you to carry a gun, leastways not one that can be seen. Fellas tend to talk more freely with fellas who ain't loaded for bear. They're apt to get a mite tetchy seeing men all armed up. Could mistake them for Judge Parker's manhunters. If you do get into trouble God's servant's strong right hand fisting a Colt will be nearby to help you out, never fear. Now let's get some shut-eye, we've got a lot of territory to cover and I ain't got many years to do it in."

7

"I'M sorry to have to tell you, but your two friends are dead and buried, sir," the manager of the Lincoln Hotel told Helman. "Shot dead in a gunfight in the Silver Dollar saloon. Another three men were also killed and the owner, Mr Sam Bigelow, was wounded in the arm."

Helman silently cursed a blue streak but somehow on the surface he remained calm. In a voice heavy with false concern he said, "Are their personal effects still in the hotel? I feel that it's beholden on me to take them back to their close kin. Something to remember their boys by."

"No sir, they aren't," the manager replied. "Why, we even had to sell their horses and saddles so that they could be decently buried."

Helman didn't give a damn if Zeb

and Stu had to be skinned and the skin sold to make moccasins with so that they could be planted in a pine box. All he was interested in was the whereabouts of their money. The sons-of-bitches couldn't have blown it all away? If it had been possible to kill Zeb and Stu twice over it would have given him great satisfaction and pleasure to do so. He resisted the strong temptation to put a bullet in the manager's hide just to ease his frustrated anger at losing half the grubstake needed to get his grand plan going.

Helman gave the hotel manager a long searching stare and opined that he was telling the truth. Zeb and Stu wouldn't have handed their pokes over to someone else to look after, they'd rather have given blood away. And if the little dude had got his greasy hands on it he wouldn't have been standing behind a desk in a fleabag hotel talking to him. He would have been long gone, back East to buy a real fancy hotel for himself. And the law hadn't got hold of the money otherwise the manager would have told him about it. That left only one alternative: someone in the Silver Dollar saloon had lifted it off Zeb and Stu's bodies.

"Thanks for seeing that they had a Christian burial," Helman said, voice still oozing false sentiment. "Now it's my sorrowful task to break the sad news to their kinfolk." He touched his hat to the manager and bade him goodnight.

Helman rein-led his horse along the street to the Silver Dollar, loose tying it on to the hitching rail. Before entering the saloon he checked the action and loads of his Colt. He was going to do some questioning inside, backed by a drawn pistol if needs be, and force out some straight answers. It could come to shooting because he had no intention of losing what rightly belonged to him without a fight. That might mean that he had to leave the saloon a damn sight faster than he was going in. His slackly tied-up horse would give him that few seconds faster getaway.

He walked straight to the bar and ordered a whiskey. While it was being poured out he conversationally said to the barkeep, "I hear that there's been some trouble in here recently?"

Being too early for the regular evening trade to come rolling in the barkeep was in a talkative mood. "Trouble, mister," he said. "It was a real war. There were bodies all over the place. One of the girls had her teeth knocked out and the boss got plugged in the arm. That's sure some trouble, friend." The barkeep grinned cockily. "I downed one of the crazy hillbillies who started the shootin'; they claimed the roulette wheel was crooked; I got him with both barrels of the shotgun under the counter here. That big bouncer sittin' playin' poker over there downed the other sonuvabitch."

"Yeah, I guess it was as you said, barkeep, a real battle," Helman said, his smile a death's head rictus, once again fighting the urge to shoot someone, the barkeep for starters, to cool down his temper. Shooting dead the men who had killed Zeb and Stu wouldn't help him to get their money back, and as sure as hell it wouldn't help Zeb and Stu. On the positive side he was closing in on the man who had Zeb and Stu's cut of the raid. Like the manager of the hotel, the barkeep and the poker-playing bouncer hadn't got their hands on it or they wouldn't still be working in the bar. But a man who fixed his roulette wheel to up the take in his saloon wouldn't think twice about taking dead men's money. The skull-like smile returned to Helman's face. He would have to say a few persuasive words in the bossman's ears, backed up by a pistol stuck in his face.

"Is the boss in, barkeep?" asked Helman.

"Big Sam?" the barkeep said. "Yeah he's in his office, that door there." The barkeep pointed to a door behind the roulette table. "But I don't think he's doin' any hirin'."

"I'll just have to see about that, won't I?" replied Helman. "He can only say no." Under his breath he added, "But that ain't likely when he knows what's coming to him if he does say no."

"What the hell are you up to, mister, bursting in my office!" Big Sam said angrily, straightening up in his chair.

Helman back-heeled the door shut and stepped close up to the desk and pushed his pistol under Big Sam's prominent beak of a nose. "I'm the man who's come for all that money you took off my two boys you had shot down."

Big Sam, even eyeballing a pistol that close, wasn't a man who scared easily. He tried to bluff it out. "I don't know what you're talking about! Yeah, my men gunned down your boys, the drunken sonsuvbitches killed three of my men, gave me this." Big Sam raised his bandaged arm from the desk, "But you'll have to look elsewhere for the money you reckon they had. Now get

outa my office before I have you . . . "
Big Sam's voice was cut off in a howl
of pain as Helman lashed him across
the wounded arm with the barrel of his
pistol.

"Don't give me that crap!" Helman
snarled, leaning across the table glaring
at Big Sam. "Or I'll work on your
busted arm real good. Fix it so no
sawbones will be able to put it together
again. Now where is the dough?"

Big Sam rocked to and fro in his chair
nursing his wounded arm. Through
tear-filled eyes he looked at Helman
and saw a man as gun-crazy as his
two buddies had been. Loco enough
to carry out his threat to mash up
his arm. "Damn it, you bastard!" he
gasped between groans. "What you're
after is in that safe!"

Helman, keeping his pistol pointing
at Big Sam, moved round the desk and
knelt down at the small safe standing
in a corner of the office. He opened
the door and reached inside, his pistol
momentarily swinging off the saloon

owner. Big Sam saw his chance. He tugged out the small hideaway pistol from the inside of his coat. At the same time as he saw that the safe only contained ledgers and papers Helman heard the squeaking of the chair behind him. He twisted round on his heels, face contorted in mad-assed rage and put a Colt shell in Big Sam's head. That the saloon owner was about to throw down on him with a derringer hadn't made him shoot Big Sam in defence of his own life, Helman had been spoiling for a killing and to find the safe empty of cash sent his temper boiling over.

The impact of the point-blank shot lifted Big Sam forward out of his chair then he slumped back, hands flopping down either side of the chair, the unfired derringer falling to the floor.

The office door suddenly burst open and the bouncer who had been pointed out to him by the barkeep rushed into the room, pistol fisted. Helman, now in a real killing mood, put a slug in his chest that pushed the bouncer back into the saloon in a heel-and-toe-shuffling gait. Helman didn't wait to see him fall, he knew that he killed him that was all that mattered. He ran across the office and slammed the door shut, this time turning the key in the lock. It would give him a few precious minutes, not to search the office for Zeb and Stu's money which he smelt was stashed somewhere in the office, the time he had got wasn't long enough for that. In a minute or two the law would come high-tailing it into the saloon, break down the door and, as disappointed as he was at having to leave Kansas City no richer, it was better than leaving the town feet first on the short, one-way trip to Boot Hill.

All chewed up, he spat a curse at Big Sam's body as he opened the rear door of the office. He cast a quick glance outside, into an alley, dark, and at the moment quiet. Turning, he fired two shots through the door leading into the saloon, to deter the opposition, and squeeze out the time he had already won a mite more. Quickly reloading the Colt he stepped out into the alley. Hurrying along it, hammer of the Colt drawn back at full-cock, he made Main Street without being challenged or shot at.

Helman eased the hammer of his pistol forward then sheathed it and stepping on to the boardwalk, strolled along to the entrance of the saloon. He joined the crowd milling round the swing doors.

"Some sort of trouble inside, mister?" he asked one of the onlookers.

"Yeah, I hear that a bouncer's been shot dead and the fella who's supposed to have done it has locked himself in Big Sam's office, with Big Sam for company," the man said. "The marshal and two shotgun deputies have just gone inside. I figure they intend blasting the shootist out."

"I'd better move my horse then," Helman said. "If there's lead goin' to be flyin' about I sure don't want it to stop any, I bought it not a couple hours ago."

Still keeping it cool Helman stepped down into the street, jerked the reins free, and mounted up and rode out of Kansas City, leaving the hornets' nest he had stirred up behind him. He had a lot to think about on his ride to Shorty Carr's Whiskey Palace. None of it happy thoughts. He hadn't the cash behind him now to buy all the cattle he knew he could get offered if the price could be quickly met. His grand scheme would have to be slowed down somewhat. It would take that much longer for him to get to the top of the pile. He fervently hoped that Zeb and Stu were suffering all the torments hell was supposed to have, adding a few more of his own to get his ill-feeling out of his system.

8

"**I**AIN'T been in a whorehouse before, Mr Simms," Cal suddenly said. Hard-eyeing the fake Reverend he truculently added, "It wasn't because I didn't hanker after havin' the pleasures of . . . " he hesitated slightly, "of, you know what I mean, Mr Simms. It was because I hadn't the two dollars to pay for a girl." There came another pause, then lowering his gaze, in a softer voice he said, "to tell the truth, Mr Simms, I ain't humped a woman for free either."

Woodrow held back his grin. Fatherly he said, "You'll be OK. You've got money now. The rest will come naturally, like sleepin' and eating, believe me."

As they neared the township of Bodie, Woodrow had suggested that Cal should start asking his questions in the local cathouse.

"It's more private than standin' at some saloon bar. Barkeeps are noted for their loose-mouthing. You know what questions to ask. You're lookin' for your cousin, Bob Helman, who rides with a 'breed Mex called Perole and two more sidekicks, Zeb and Stu. Don't push the questioning, make it kinda casual," Woodrow grinned. "And don't let the questioning spoil your pleasure: you enjoy yourself, don't waste my two dollars. Don't seek me out, I'll be close by. I don't want anyone to link us together. The Nations is full of suspicious-minded, hair-triggered *hombres*." It wasn't only the bad-asses Woodrow was worried about. He could get fingered by a badge-toting man, a long shot he had to admit. But long shots sometimes come in and he didn't want the kid to be dragged into his trouble.

★ ★ ★

"Well, Cal, ain't you or ain't you not gonna take off your clothes?" Beth said, irritably. "You ain't payin' for an all-nighter."

Cal gazed round-eyed at Beth, a brunette about his own age, lying stretched out on the bed wearing only her fancy, lace-trimmed red drawers and a frilly garter on her right leg. Cal had expected some fooling around first, kissing and squeezing, m'be with his coat off but the speed with which Beth had shucked what few clothes she had on caught him off balance, embarrassed him. He could no longer feel the blood racing round his body, its pounding at his temples making him think that it was about to burst out of his ears. He stood there as though in a trance, too tongue-tied to answer Beth.

More bold-assed than he was feeling Cal had walked into the cathouse like some tall-in-the-saddle, horn dog, top hand, well dressed, well heeled, being told by Mr Simms that folk would generally answer questions from a soberly-dressed man than one looking like a saddle-bum.

Cal strode into the grandest furnished room he had ever seen with thick, purple-coloured drapes at the windows, and a blue carpet as deep and soft as summer prairie grass. And the girls. They were something. It was then that his blood began to race. They were lounging about on red-hide settees and chairs, half-naked, showing practically all they were offering. Before he lost his nerve at their bold mocking-grins and ran out of the room he took hold of one of the girls and led her to the plump-assed, slack-breasted madam sitting at a table near the foot of the stairs and, without speaking, paid her his two dollars and hurried his choice up the stairs. Before the girl took him into her room he blurted out, "My name is Cal, what's yours, miss?"

Beth pulled Cal close to her, feeling that she could enjoy being humped by Cal. He was young, not bad-looking, didn't smell like a hog, and was stone-cold sober. She gave him a smile that, most unprofessionally, reached her eyes. "I'm Beth," she said. Cal had looked into her inviting eyes and almost forgot what he had really come into the cathouse for. Forgot what day it was.

And now he was standing gawking at her all dead inside when a couple of minutes back he was all burning up. Softly Beth said, "Ain't I worth two silver dollars, Cal?" And began wriggling out of her drawers. Cal's inhibitions vanished in another wave of blood-pounding heat. By heck, he thought, worth two dollars? If he owned the Nations he would give Beth half. He quickly peeled off his clothes.

Madame Lily sat deep in thought. She had smelt something phoney about the kid Beth had gone upstairs with. He had been extra nervous. That wasn't natural, she thought, for even a first-timer in a cathouse. It was something she couldn't pinpoint but her instincts had never let her down before. It paid Madame Lily to check out her clients who weren't her regulars real well. She ran an extra service in the cathouse, equally as lucrative as the main business of the house, though not so legal. Two rooms at the rear of the house were never used by the girls and their clients. They were for special, backdoor entry clients. Men who were running ahead of a hanging posse. Men who had a pressing need to lie low for a spell, and the wherewithal to do it in comfort. Madame Lily had two such clients occupying one of the rooms right now, the Clancy brothers. Men wanted for armed robbery and three counts of murder in Texas and New Mexico.

The kid, she conceded, could be just who he looked like, a hayseed in town from the sticks. But the Clancys were paying her good money to make sure that they got an early warning if any one who even smelt like the law came nosing around. The kid was definitely not one of Judge Parker's hard-assed marshals but he could be a Pinkerton. The Pinkerton Detective Agency had young, smooth-faced men working for them. Pussyfooting around the Territory seeking out men the official law couldn't track down. Madame Lily heaved her bulk out of the chair and waddled upstairs to the back rooms. The Clancy boys could take it from here, she opined.

Cal was putting his clothes back on, wearing a cat's-got-the-cream grin of supreme contentment, eyeing the still jay-bird naked Beth lying on the bed smiling back at him. He contemplated spending two more dollars to have another session with Beth but regretfully decided against it. It was no good overdoing it in the first whorehouse he visited. There must be hundreds of suchlike sporting houses in the Nations and Mr Simms could run out of money before they cut Helman's sign. His grin reached his ears. And he didn't want to end up bushed with overindulgence.

Instead he told Beth of his searching for his cousin, Helman, who supposedly was somewhere here in the Nations. He drew a blank from her.

"But I'll ask the other girls for you, Cal," Beth said. "They might have heard where your cousin is. I've just arrived here from Kansas, I don't know anyone at all. And Madame Lily could m'be help you out, this is a popular house."

Cal had been told to be discreet in his questioning and he thought that spreading the word all over the whorehouse didn't seem to be the best way to do that. "It's OK, Beth," he said. "I'll ask around in the bars."

Beth rolled off the bed and began to get dressed, which did little to lower the temperature of Cal's blood. The sight of the tight, smooth curves of her breasts and ass made him say a hurried farewell and he almost ran out of the room before he lost the will to resist her charms.

* * *

Woodrow sat at the window table of Mrs Kendrew's Tea Shoppe drinking pale-coloured tea from an eggshell cup, smiling man-of-God-like benignly at the six bonneted elderly ladies partaking of the same beverage at a nearby table. He was also keeping a watchful eye on the cathouse hoping that the kid wouldn't be long in showing up. He couldn't go on keeping up the pretence of enjoying the piss he was downing much longer and there was the risk that the old biddies would engage him in small-talk about religious matters.

He was much relieved to see Cal come out of the cathouse, stand on the steps for a few moments as though deciding what he should do next, then walk off along the street to the saloon section of the town. He watched Cal cross the alley between the cathouse and a general dealer's store, wondering if the kid had been lucky and had got a lead on Helman at first try. Woodrow smiled. He hoped also the kid had got his full two dollars' worth of pleasure. When this business was settled he would speculate a few dollars himself to enjoy himself likewise. He wasn't too old to climb on top of a young whore yet, he hoped, being that it had been quite a spell since he had done so. He got answering smiles from the tea ladies and thought that they would choke on their cream cakes if they knew what he was smiling about.

He glanced out of the window again and the kid was no longer in sight. He wouldn't have had time to have reached the store door, let alone gone inside to question the storekeeper about Helman if he had that in mind. Woodrow's old owlhoot's inner senses began to twitch. Someone had taken him into the side alley, with or without the kid's consent. Hurriedly he got to his feet. With a skin-deep mask of a smile as his excuse me to the ladies he left the tearoom and stepped smartly across the street, no longer smiling.

"Does the little runt smell like a Pinkerton to you, Pete?" Cal heard the big, black-whiskered man growl. "Lily seems to think he's more than he seems to be."

A frightened-faced Cal looked up at his burly accuser who had suddenly grabbed him by the scruff of his neck and dragged him into the alley.

"Could be, Butch," his pardner replied, a thin stoat-visaged man, as he close-eyed Cal. He bared broken teeth in a mirthless grin that chilled Cal's blood. "Why don't you ask the kid right out if he's a Pinkerton snooper, Butch?"

Butch's smile was less comforting to Cal than Pete's had been. "I was just about to do that, Pete," he said, and brought his fist sweeping across in a round-handed blow against the side of Cal's head.

Unprepared for it Cal caught the full force of the savage blow. His teeth rattled in his skull as he bounced against the cathouse wall. Bells rang

103

loudly in his ears and he tasted the saltiness of blood in his mouth. Still grinning, Butch said, "That's just a piece of what to expect if you give us any forked-tongue talk about your business here." He raised a threatening, ham-like fist.

Cal did some rapid thinking. If the two were Helman's boys why were they not asking him what he wanted to see Helman for before beating him up? And how had they picked on him so quickly? If they weren't riding with Helman what had made them think that he was a Pinkerton? He stopped trying to figure out why he was being pushed into a tight corner, it was only making the pain in his head worse but stubborn mulish pride gave him the courage to stand up to the big man. Glaring mad-eyed at him he painfully mouthed, "I ain't no Pinkerton you big gorilla. I've just been in the cathouse for a hump. Ain't been in the town more than a few hours, and mindin' my own business."

Butch stayed his hand. "What do you think, Pete? Is the little squirt tellin' the truth?"

"I think that you two gents should leave the boy alone and go about your own business," Woodrow said.

Cal leaned back against the wall and breathed a sigh of relief at Woodrow's appearance. He had said that he would be close by, though Cal wished that the old fart had been closer so that he could have showed up before the big bastard had bounced him around.

Butch gave another one of his fierce smiles. "Well, lookee here, Pete, a sky-pilot. Let me give you a piece of advice, preacher-man go about your own business and let me get on with my discussion with the kid here. Or as sure as hell I'll pull out my hogleg and shoot your goddamned ears off."

You're riding for a fall, mister, Cal thought, hoping that he would get the chance to shake the big man's brains around somewhat.

"Well ain't you goin' to leave the

boy alone, or do I have to force you to back off?" Woodrow said, still soft-voiced.

"He's scarin' me now, Pete," Butch said. "Is he scarin' you?"

Pete's smile was as toothy and savage as Butch's. "If you're too scared to draw on him I'll plug him for you, Butch."

"The pleasure's mine, Pete," replied Butch. "I ain't shot a preacher before." His hand reached down for the pistol at his hip.

Woodrow's hand flashed to his coat lapels.

Cal had seen a gun come into action as fast before, at the stagecoach he had attempted to rob, when the same gun was stuck under his nose. He had never seen two men killed so speedily before, so fast and unexpected that it sent him leaning back against the wall again, all shook up and sick inside at the sight of the blood-streaming head wounds. He knew the pair were riding for a fall when they foolishly faced Mr Simms but he hadn't expected them to drop all the way to hell.

Woodrow came up to him. Seeing his white, staring-eyed face he growled. "What the hell was I supposed to do, Mr Lewis? Preach them a sermon? Wing 'em? One thing you've got to know, kid, especially if you're gonna take up robbin' stages, if someone pulls a gun on you, it's too late for doing any talkin'. You heave yours out and down him first, and for keeps. A wounded man can kill you just as surely as one who ain't." Woodrow took a closer look at the men he had shot. "They're not part of the bunch I'm seekin', kid. Unless Helman's started hirin'. And I reckon we won't have time to find out. Again they could be characters naturally suspicious of strangers in town."

Woodrow heard shouts from the street and the sound of running footsteps on the boardwalk. He pulled Cal's pistol from its holster and slipped it in his pocket, putting his own gun into a surprised Cal's hand. "Now look as though you've just downed two men who, for some unknown reason, pulled guns on you," he said.

A bunch of men came running at the sight of the two bodies lying in the alley.

"I saw the shootin', Marshal," Woodrow said to a little stubby man with a lawman's badge pinned to his vest. He introduced himself. "The Reverend Joshua Simms, Officer," he said, then continued with his lying. "These two men were beating up this young man and I tried to stop them. They drew their guns on me and were going to shoot me. This brave boy, at risk of his own life, drew his own pistol and shot them dead. As much as I abhor the taking of human life, even evil sinners like those two must have been, the boy had no choice, unless he was prepared to see me lying there instead of those two." Woodrow gave the marshal an oily, sanctimonious smile. "There but for the grace of God . . . "

The marshal tugged at the end of his straggling longhorn moustache as he gimlet-eyed Woodrow. Then he looked at Cal, seeing the blood on his chin, then at the dead men's pistols lying in the dirt alongside them.

"It happened just like the reverend said, Marshal," Cal said. "I couldn't just stand here and let them shoot him down like a dog."

The marshal switched his gaze back on to Cal again. "How come they were beatin' you up, kid?"

"I don't know, Marshal," replied Cal. "I ain't seen them before. Ain't been in town more than a couple hours. They musta been drunks spoilin' for a fight I reckon."

The marshal grunted. "It looks like an open-and-shut case of self-defence so I'd be obliged if you could put your Colt away." The kid, by the look of him he thought, was still uptight after gunning down two men and nervous reaction could make him pull the trigger again and he was in direct line of fire.

"Of course you'll have to come along to my office to sign papers to that effect."

"Yeah, sure Marshal," Cal said, as he sheathed his pistol.

"I'd be obliged if you would do the same, Reverend, to witness the statement," the marshal said. With the toe of his boot he turned one of the bodies face uppermost. "Well I'll be durned!" he exclaimed. He turned to Cal. "These two characters are the Clancy boys wanted for murder and robberies in three states. You've put them where they should have been before they were britched. And collected yourself the two thousand dollars bounty Wells Fargo have put on their heads, dead or alive. It might take a week or so for your money to come through but it's yours, kid. Now let's get along to my office and I can wire the Wells Fargo head office in Kansas your details, your name where you're puttin' up etcetera."

Cal glanced across at Woodrow. "I'm

not stayin' long in Bodie, Marshal," he said. "I've been offered a job on a ranch in Texas, my uncle's spread. But the offer's only open for a week so if I don't show up soon he'll hire someone else. While two thousand dollars is a right fine sum of money for a young kid like me to get presented with it ain't as good as holdin' down a regular job of work." Cal reckoned he could lie as smoothly as the phoney preacher he was hitched to could.

"You ride down to Texas, kid," the marshal said. "Get yourself signed on the payroll. I'll have the reward money paid in at the bank here. You can pick it up at your own convenience. It's good to see a younker thinkin' sensibly, not wantin' to blow his windfall on gamblin', drinkin' and the pleasurin' of lewd women. Ain't that so, Reverend?"

The reverend smiled and nodded.

Cal and Woodrow had both penned their signatures to the required statements and were told by the marshal that they were free to leave town whenever they wished.

"You're doin' right not waitin' around for your money, Mr Lewis," the marshal said. "The shootin' coulda excited some of the young bloods who fancy themselves as up-and-comin' *pistoleros* into callin' you out. Then there's other folk on hearin' that you've come into big money will become real friendly-like towards you, till they've helped you to spend it all. Ain't that the truth, Reverend?"

Woodrow gave another agreeing smile. Piously he said, "Unfortunately so, Marshal. Greed and jealousy are all around us in spite of the good work the church is doing. Now, if you would both excuse me I must be on my way." He shook hands with Cal. "Thank you my son for saving the life of one of the Lord's servants. I will pray that you will come to no harm when you begin your new life in Texas. I'm travelling that way myself. If you are leaving now as well, perhaps we could travel together, it would help to break up the

112

monotony of the trail. Spreading the Lord's word is a heart-breaking, lonely task sometimes, Marshal."

It was the marshal's turn to nod his head in agreement. Taking account of the sin and wickedness that was going on in Bodie it was also a waste of good horse flesh riding around the Territory spouting words about spreading the gospel.

* * *

Once clear of Bodie Woodrow expressed his thoughts on the recent happenings. "Mr Lewis," he said. "You can quit. I put you in a dangerous situation, could have got yourself killed. The deal don't run to that. You've got some money behind you, you're entitled to live to enjoy spendin' it."

"I made the deal, Mr Simms," Cal said. "That was the third time you got me out of a tight corner. So I'm beholden to you." Cal grinned. "Besides I reckon I could get a likin' payin' visits to cathouses."

"It ain't so joyful for me, kid," Woodrow growled good-naturedly, "if I've got to shoot men dead outside every one you visit. We'll stay clear of suchlike places, pay a call on Belle Starr at Younger's Bend. I didn't intend payin' her a visit but the way things turned out in Bodie it's the healthiest option."

9

AS they breasted a long, high ridge Cal saw the sheen of a creek that snaked its tortuous way across the flat. In the middle distance, on the nearside of one of the twists of the creek, he picked out a raggedy spread of buildings and corrals and a large single-storeyed, porch-fronted big house.

"That's Younger's Bend, Mr Lewis," Woodrow said. "Home of Mrs Belle Starr, the toughest female in the Nations, and elsewhere for that matter. Though I heard when I was inside that Bob Starr had got himself shot dead in a dance-hall ruckus. So Belle must be a widow woman now. Unless she's got hitched again. She never did like sleepin' on her own." He gave Cal a big brother, caring look. "Just in case Belle comes on strong for you I ought to warn you that Belle's fellas have the unhealthy habit of either getting themselves dead or plugged full of holes and thrown in jail for a long spell like poor Coleman Younger."

Cal, remembering the feel of Beth's firm, smooth body didn't think that Mrs Belle Starr, who would definitely be no spring chicken, could stir his blood the way Beth had.

"It ain't much of a place, Younger's Bend, is it, Mr Simms?" he said. "I was expectin' a settlement, a small town m'be. It ain't nothin' but a holdin'. And it sure doesn't look a money-makin' one at that."

"Younger's Bend was Belle's fancy name for the place," replied Woodrow. "I'll agree it ain't much to gaze on now but one time or another under that roof sat the most sought after law-breakers in the Midwest?" He grinned. "Yours truly bein' one of them. Belle kinda hits the bottle hard when the mood's on her, tends to make her loose-mouthed so leave all the talkin' to me about the reason we're in the Nations, OK?"

On hearing the sound of riders coming up to her house Belle Starr came out on to the porch curious to see who her unexpected visitors were. More than likely, she thought, they would be drifters looking for a handout to tide them on their way or m'be deputy marshals working out of Fort Smith on the trail for some two-bit bad-hat. All the owlhooters who had rattled their spurs across this porch were long gone.

Blue Duck, sitting on the far end of the porch, idly thinking that he should be riding south to the border with the gang Helman must have raised by now if Belle had not threatened to track him down and put two loads of birdshot in his hide, got to his feet and like Belle watched the two riders close in on the house. He nervously fingered the butt of his holstered Colt his thoughts now more concentrated on whether he had still unserved warrants out on him and the two men were marshals riding in to serve them.

"Well as I live and breathe! One of them is that old fart, Woodrow!" he heard Belle gasp out in astonishment.

Cal saw a middle-aged, hatchet-faced woman with a belted pistol across her middle. The long, ankle-length dress, made of some red material, did nothing to make her look feminine. It was as he had thought, she wasn't a woman he would like to share a bed with. Though, he opined, he had no right to be choosy, after all the only woman he had had cost him two dollars. And it looked like she was no longer a widow woman. The shifty-eyed, thin-pencil moustached man, about his age, he reckoned, must be Belle Starr's latest bed pardner. He was favouring him and Mr Simms with a tough-hombre's fish-eyed glare.

"Ain't you gonna ask me and my *compadre*, Mr Lewis, here, to step down, Belle?" Woodrow said. "Or ain't there any hospitality at Younger's Bend nowadays?"

"Of course there's hospitality here,

you old coot," Belle said, grinning with pleasure. "It's just that I ain't invited a preacher inside my house before. Step down the pair of you." She gave Woodrow a quizzical look. "When did you get religion, Woody, in San Quentin?"

Woodrow smiled. "I ain't what I'm dressed like, Belle," he said, as he and Cal swung down from their mounts. "It's just that I'm kinda touchy about the law knowin' I'm in the Nations." He gave Blue Duck a pointed look.

"Oh!" Belle exclaimed. "I'm neglectin' my manners. You've never met Blue Duck, have you Woody?"

Woodrow, like Cal, wasn't impressed by Blue Duck's looks. He gave him a curt nod thinking that Belle was going for weak-chinned, baby-faced kids now. "I heard about Bob in the Pen, getting himself killed. There ain't only but a few of the old guns left, Belle."

"Ain't that the truth, Woody," said Belle. "Though to be fair, that asshole of a drunk, Bob Starr, was askin' for what he finally got. Now Cole Younger," Belle sighed nostalgically, "he was one real hell-raiser. But he could treat a woman like a real city swell." Belle smiled. "Enough of this gabbin', come on inside, you as well, Mr Lewis, and I'll fix you both some chow. Then you can tell me what's been happenin' to you, preacher man. Blue Duck can see to the horses."

Cal grinned as Blue Duck, scowling-faced, took hold of his mount's reins. He opined that Mrs Belle Starr wore the pants at Younger's Bend. He also had the confident feeling that if Blue Duck, Indian-named or not, tried to crowd him he could make him back off with no sweat at all. He also got to wondering just who the hell the man was who called himself the Reverend Joshua Simms. Belle Starr was calling him Woody. If he was willing to ride alongside a man, getting beat up for, Cal reckoned that it was only right and proper for that man to tell him his real name.

After a meal, which Cal had to admit that though Belle may be no beauty she sure was one hell of a cook, Woodrow asked Belle if she had heard of a man called Helman hiding out in the Nations.

Belle, smoking a long black cigarello, shook her head. "It ain't a name I recollect being mentioned in this part of the Territory, Woody. Have you some deal goin' on with this fella?"

Woodrow smiled thinly. "Yeah, I've got business with him, Belle. Urgent business, settling up business."

And Belle, plainswoman that she was, knew it wasn't polite to ask even an old friend like Woodrow just what that cold-smiling business was.

"I saw this fella, Helman, you're askin' about," Blue Duck said. "M'be a couple weeks back, rode in Shorty Carr's place."

"Shorty Carr's? Where does he hang out?" Woodrow asked, all alert.

"Shorty showed up in the Nations after you went inside, Woody," Belle told him. "Sells coal-oil whiskey out of a shack along the Turtle Creek trail. He also makes a few dollars on the side by passing on messages from one party to another when the parties concerned are shy about showing themselves in towns to send Western Union wires."

"He had a 'breed Mex with him," Blue Duck put in. "Asked Shorty to seek some men out for him, men who can handle cattle. Then he rode off someplace, so did the 'breed. But he rode south, Helman headed Kansas way. I reckon by now he's back and picked up the men he wanted. If it's cattle he's interested in and he's moved out, it must be south. The way the 'breed took."

"Well I'll be durned," Woodrow said. His longshot had come romping home. "Was there two other men, young kids, with Helman and the 'breed?" he asked Blue Duck.

"Only the two of them showed up at Shorty's," Blue Duck replied.

Belle Starr laughed. "You ain't

thinkin' about goin' into the cattle trade, Woody? Why you don't know the ass end of a longhorn from the end the grass is stuffed in."

Woodrow's face steeled over, his eyes focusing on how future events could be unfolding. "No I ain't Belle. As I said, it's gettin' even business I have with Helman." His face softened and he brought his gaze back on to Belle. "I've a feelin' that I'm comin' close to seein' my business settled up, favourin' me."

"I don't know, Woody," Belle said. "Texas is a mighty big place. A whole army could lose itself in that hellhole of a land. And it ain't a place where a man can go askin' the whereabouts of other men without riskin' a big Colt .45 slug in his hide for bein' so nosy. Dressed in a sky-pilot's gear or not. And you needn't make me feel uncomfortable any longer sitting at my table dressed like that. I've heard of no warrants being put out on you in the Nations, Woody. And if you intend riding below the Brazos, why, there ain't no law there at all."

Blue Duck spoke again. "M'be I can help you out. I know men along the Texas trails. My askin' for this fella Helman won't attract the trouble a stranger askin' the same question would."

Belle gave her latest beau a calculating look. She knew that Blue Duck had itchy feet. Wanted to ride out of Younger's Bend to try and make a name for himself as a wild-assed *pistolero*. But what he said made sense, and she was beholden, from long friendship and old times' sake, to help Woody in his settling-up business all she could. She looked back at Woody. "What Blue Duck says sounds good, Woody. Could save you a lot of time and a heap of grief."

Woodrow chewed over Blue Duck's offer for a minute or so. His judgement of him was that he wasn't a man who would do someone a good turn just to be charitable. He had made the offer for some personal reason of his own. As long as he kept a tight rein on him, he thought, Blue Duck could do him no harm. He shot a glance at Cal, seeing by the expression on his face that he was having the same feelings regarding Blue Duck's unsolicited offer. He gave Cal a quick, understanding wink then said, "Me and my pard will be pleased to have you ride alongside us, Blue Duck. We'll move out before noon tomorrow, if that's OK with you, Belle."

"It's fine by me, Woody," replied Belle. "Now the business is over let's get down to serious drinkin' and tell me what the hell you've been up to, Woody, since the last time you had your legs under this table."

Cal stood up. "Being all the talk will be about happenin's long before I was born I think I'll go to bed." Po-faced he added, "I'm a young man and I need my sleep, especially after eatin' some of the best cooked chow I've ever tasted, Mrs Starr."

Belle smiled fondly. "Why thank you, Mr Lewis, it's real nice of you to say so. If you were stayin' here a mite longer m'be I could show you how good I was at other things." She burst out laughing. "Ain't that so, Woody?"

"Coleman Younger thought so, Belle," Woodrow said. He grinned as Cal, face bright red, left the room. His grin faded as he saw Blue Duck's pinched-ass scowl. Woodrow, he told himself, that *hombre* has the look of a back-shooter about him. He will definitely need watching on the trail.

One hour later, Cal, lying on his cot, still awake, thinking of the eager thrusting, clinging Beth had his pleasant thoughts broken into by Woodrow coming into the bedroom.

"You don't seem to have much to talk about," he said. "I didn't expect you comin' in till first light."

Woodrow gave him a drunk's unfocused-eyed look. "We ain't got warmed up yet. I just came in, now that things seem to be comin' to a head,

126

just to tell you who I am and why I'm huntin' down Helman. I'm Woodrow Liddell, started my robbin' along with the James and the Younger boys. I did a long stretch in San Quentin. When I came out I was foolish enough to think I could pull off one last train heist so as to set me up in comfort for the rest of my natural. I needed that sonuvabitch, Helman and his boys to help me to pull it off." Woodrow smiled, a grin as lopsided as his gaze. "Robbin' a Canadian Pacific flyer ain't like robbin' a stage." Face Indianing over he told Cal how the raid had turned out. "I had nothin' to do with the killin's, kid, and that's the truth; ain't ever killed anyone all the robbin' I done. But I don't reckon the law will see it that way. That's neither here nor there. All I'm after is settling the score with Helman and his boys, and grabbing all of the takings. So there you have it, kid. We're goin' up against hard men, killin' men, so I won't be offended if you want to call our deal off being that

I've got Blue Duck to do the askin' for me now."

Cal thought that it was a big jump for a man trying his hand at robbing a stage to get himself a grubstake to find himself as a pardner of a man whose name had been listed on wanted flyers as prominent as the Younger boys had been. And resting his head in the most notorious thieves' kitchen this side of the gates of hell. Just to make what he had landed himself in more hairy, tomorrow he was going to help track down a bunch of cold-blooded killers. Yet, surprising himself, he said, "I'm still in, Mr Woodrow. Now you get back to Mrs Starr and your reminiscing and let me get some sleep."

Woodrow grinned and gripped his shoulders. "You're OK, kid, and that's a fact. We'll pull through all right, you'll see." He raised his voice. "Belle, get that other bottle opened," he shouted, "it's howlin' at the moon time!" and staggered out of the room.

Cal dropped off to sleep hoping that

he would live long enough for him to think back on his past life. Hoping that the leap he had taken wouldn't land him alongside Butch and Pete in Boot Hill.

Sometime during the night something woke him up. It was still dark. From the far corner of the room he heard Woodrow's cot creaking and groaning, then Belle Starr's giggling laugh ending in a small but joyous cry of, "Woody, don't make a hog of yourself, get to sleep."

Cal grinned in the dark. Facing Helman and his gang didn't seem to be cramping Woody's style. He fell asleep again confident that one day he would be telling his grandchildren of how he rode with Mr Woodrow Liddell, the greatest train-heister in the south-west.

★ ★ ★

They were ready to move out. Each of them leading a well-laden packhorse.

Belle, standing on the porch to see them leave, had insisted that they should be well-stocked up for their journey.

"So long, Belle," Woodrow said. "And thanks." He grinned down at her from his saddle. "For everything. I may swing back this way when me and Helman have settled up our differences."

"I'll hold you to that, you old goat," a tearful Belle said. "Take care now, there ain't many of us old 'uns left. And you too Mr Lewis. You're ridin' with a *bueno hombre*, kid."

Woodrow touched his hat in a final farewell gesture to Belle then he said. "OK, boys, let's move out. We'll pay a call on this fella Shorty Carr, he may be able to tell us some more about Helman's business than we know right now."

Woodrow halted his small column well short of Carr's Whiskey Palace and gave it a good searching look through his army glasses. He had discarded his preacher's gear and wore a pistol openly, belted about his middle. He also had another Colt in a holster under his left armpit. Along with the booted Winchester he had a shortened double-barrelled shotgun tucked loosely, for quick withdrawal, in his bedroll packed behind his saddle. He wanted all the edge he could get when he finally came face to face with Helman. He lowered the glasses.

"There's only one horse and a couple mules in the corral, Blue Duck," he said. "So it could be as you said, Helman's got his crew and on his way to where he's bound for. Or he ain't showed up yet. So I reckon it's safe for us to ride down there and have words with Mr Shorty Carr." Woodrow favoured Blue Duck with a cold-eyed grin. "When I meet up with Helman I want it to be a surprise. I ain't so fast with a gun, or blowhard enough to think that I can take him backed by ten or twelve men."

Shorty Carr, standing on his porch, gave them a saloon-owner's paste-thick

131

welcoming smile as they drew up outside the Palace.

"Howdy Blue Duck," he said. "If you and your buddies have come to sign on with Mr Helman, you've ridden over here for nothin'. He left with all the men he needed four days ago." Shorty's grin widened. "Ten of the most evil-dispositioned *hombres* I've ever clapped eyes on who weren't swingin' under some tree with hemp collars round their necks."

"Any idea where Helman was makin' for, Mr Carr?" Woodrow said. "M'be I can catch up with him and persuade him to take me and my boy here on his payroll."

"Mr Helman was a tight-lipped, ugly, mean sonuvabitch when he first showed up here," said Shorty. "When he came back, I heard later he'd been to Kansas City, he was meaner lookin' than the meanest blood-crazy Comanche. Something or someone had upset him real bad in Kansas City. And it wasn't woman trouble. Helman had the cut of a man who wouldn't shed tears over the deathbed of his own mother. When Perole returned and Helman had words with him he got the same kinda upset look. When they rode out, they rode south. And that's all I know, mister."

Neither Blue Duck or Shorty had mentioned Zeb and Stu, Woodrow thought, so he reckoned that the news that had soured Helman's face was linked with their non-appearance at Shorty's. The pair for some reason had broken with him. Helman would naturally be upset at losing half of his gang. Especially when he had this cattle scheme of his rolling. M'be the pair weren't prepared to put some of their share of the takings up front to finance Helman's new venture. Whatever, it was bad news for him also. Once he had tracked Helman and Perole down he would have to start a fresh hunt for Zeb and Stu. On his own, if he was still above ground. He couldn't expect the kid to continue risking his life on what was a private vendetta. He faced Blue

Duck. "Where would you go," he said, "if you wanted to get into the cattle business on the cheap?"

Blue Duck thought for a minute or two. "The cheapest way is to lift someone else's beef. But that ain't a healthy occupation in Texas. In Mexico there ain't the same risk of gettin' strung up for cattle rustlin' and the askin' price for longhorns is cheaper. Most of them bein' *gringo* beef stoled by the Comanche or the Apache. They end up bein' sold to the Comancheros, Mex *bandidos*, for trade whiskey and guns. If a man has the balls to set up a meetin' with those wild hombres he could get hold of some real cheap cattle for good Yankee dollars."

Woodrow cursed. "Trackin' down Helman across northern Mexico ain't goin' to be easy." He eyeballed Blue Duck. "Unless you've got some buddies livin' along the Rio Grande, amigo?"

"I know men along the border who would know if so much as a rat swims across the Rio Grande."

Woodrow's face brightened up. "Mr Blue Duck," he said. "I'm right pleased that you offered to come along. Me and Mr Lewis would have been wanderin' all over the Territory like two lost kids tryin' to find Helman. Let's head for the Rio Grande, you take the point again, Blue Duck."

Woodrow waited till Blue Duck was several horse lengths ahead of them on the trail then he drew up his horse and waited for Cal to come alongside him. Leaning across his saddle he said, "Keep a wary eye on that fella ahead, Mr Lewis. I don't trust him. If he makes a move against us, plug him! Savvy?" He smiled. "Not for keeps, or you'll have Belle Starr chasin' after you with a shotgun."

Cal swallowed hard. He'd had some firsts in the last week or so. First attempt at robbing a stage, first ride in a tumbleweed wagon, first beating-up. And now the grim, frightening possibility of having to fire his gun in anger. The one pleasant first time, the humping of Beth, in no way made up for the scary events. He hoped morbidly, that his short time with Beth wasn't going to be his last as well as his first time he would enjoy having a woman. Then again, he had only himself to blame for what could happen to him in the future, Mr Liddell had offered him a way out. Cal gritted his teeth. First time or not, he would shoot down Blue Duck for sure if the shifty-eyed son-of-a-bitch had evil intentions against him and Mr Liddell. He wasn't going to prevent him having more fun out of life than he'd had up till now. He kneed his horse forward to follow along behind Woodrow.

10

THEY came ass-kicking out of the arroyo, whooping and yipping, like an Apache warband closing in for the kill. Helman and his men jumped up from the campfire and grabbed their rifles as the riders thundered up to the camp, threatening to ride right through it. Then the Mexican *bandidos* dragged their mounts to a haunch-sliding, dust-raising stop just short of the *gringos'* camp. Through the billowing, throat-gagging dust that enveloped the camp Helman saw the wide-grinning Perole among the riders.

"Relax boys," he said. "These greaser bastards, though they don't look like it, are friendly." Fingers eased off triggers but Helman's crew didn't loosen up all the way. They still remained standing, warily eyeing the Mexicans with their rifles held across their chests.

First point to the greasers, Helman thought angrily, for frightening the shit out of the *gringos*. Carlos, the son-of-a-bitch who bossed over the ragged-assed bunch, was deliberately showing him his strength. He had come here to do a deal with Carlos but if he kept up his stompin'-man's tactics the only thing they would be dealing in would be Winchester and Colt lead. Perole, being his cousin, could keep him in line, but he wouldn't bet on it. The chance of getting hold of some Yankee *dinero* could make Carlos see the sense of conducting business in a less hairy fashion.

The new Helman gang had made good progress making the Rio Grande, though Helman was still sour-gutted about the loss of Zeb and Stu's financial input in his deal. To make up for the shortfall in the cattle he had originally hoped to buy Helman was considering lifting beef off some of the smaller Texas ranchers. But the more he thought about the idea the more it seemed bad thinking. Although he was satisfied with the men he had hired in the Nations they weren't really a gang yet, willing to accept his sayso. They might not take kindly to him involving them in rustling Texan cattle. A man may risk his neck robbing a bank or a stage but to take a chance of getting strung up for stealing as much as one flea-ridden longhorn a man would have to be real desperate for money. And he didn't want to raise trouble for himself in Texas. He was going to deal in cattle in Texas as legally as the next rancher. In Mexico he was prepared to shoot men down if it brought cheap beef his way.

Perole had crossed the Rio Grande two days earlier to make contact with his cousin, Carlos, who ran a small bunch of grandmother's-throat-cutters in Northern Chihuahua.

"There's a village one day's ride from this crossing," Perole said. "Take your time gettin' there. It'll take me a few days to locate Carlos. There could be *rurale* patrols out along the border forcing Carlos to lie low."

"You are still on speakin' terms with your cousin?" Helman said, doubtfully. "The boys we've hired are expectin' to move cattle, not to have a gunfight with a bunch of Mexican bad-asses."

Perole grinned. "We ain't exactly kissin' cousins but Carlos won't slit your throat till he hears out the deal you're puttin' to him. He's always keen to get hold of a few extra bucks."

Perole dismounted and walked towards the fire, a pot-bellied Mexican wearing the stained and tattered remains of a *rurale* captain's uniform, crowned by a droopy-brimmed *sombrero* following along behind him. Helman noted along with the Winchester the Mexican was holding in his right hand, he also was a two pistol man. One on his right hip, the other stuck in the top of his pants. To complete his armoury he had two bandoleers of Winchester shells slung across his shoulders. Helman got to wondering how the Mexican's scrawny pony didn't buckle under the weight. He couldn't see any family likeness but he reckoned that the Mexican was Carlos, Perole's cousin.

Perole, still grinning, said, "This is my cousin, Carlos, *jefe* of this band of *hombres*. Carlos, this is my *compadre*, Helman."

Piggy eyes set in deep folds of a fat, pock-marked, unshaven face stared unblinkingly at Helman. The thick-lipped mouth opened in a wide, gold-teeth-showing smile that lacked any warmth and friendliness.

"Welcome to *Mejico, gringo*," Carlos said. "My cousin tells me that you are here to buy cattle."

Helman's smile matched Carlos's in insincerity as he felt that it would give him great pleasure to blow the *bandido jefe's* gold teeth through the back of his head. "That's why I'm here in this dog-shit land," he said. "I'll buy all the beef I can get, at a fair price."

Helman saw the beady-eyes flash

momentarily and guessed with satisfaction that he had touched Carlos on a raw spot. The *gringos* had evened up.

"I have other *gringos* who want to buy my cattle," Carlos said. "I'll have to . . ."

Helman cut Carlos's words off by turning his back on him and speaking to his men. "Boys, break up camp, let's ride back to Texas. We've hard-assed it all the way here for nothin'. This *hombre* don't want to trade with us."

"Do not be so hasty, amigo," Carlos spluttered, seeing *gringo* dollars about to slip from his grip. His paunchy face tightened up in a twisted mask of an apologetic smile. "I did not say I would not trade with you but here in *Mejico* it is the custom to spend some time discussing business. Sit down, drink a little tequila, talk over the price you're willing to pay, and what I'm willing to sell at. You *gringos* are in too much of a hurry in your dealings."

Helman thought damn right he was in a hurry. The longer he stayed in

Mexico the greater the temptation for the little fat cut-throat to try and put one over on him. Their gear, horses and guns would be a big enough prize for Carlos to try for, if it wouldn't cost him too many dead. If he got a smell of the amount of money he was carrying he would gladly sacrifice every mother's son in his gang to grab it. Even if Carlos was Perole's loving pa he wouldn't give him an inch of edge. To do so was asking for an early death.

"We *gringos* like to get our deals settled first," he said. "Then we do our drinkin'. Liquored-up men sometimes make promises they don't mean and when they sober up they rat on their pards." He hard-eyed Carlos. "I sure wouldn't like our partnership to end up in a shoot-out, *amigo*. I'll give you a dollar a head more for the beef than you're pullin' in now for the stolen *gringo* cattle. And I'll take all you can deliver." Helman saw the small eyes light up again.

"You have the money with you, *señor*, to pay for all these cattle you want?"

Señor now, thought Helman, the son-of-a-bitch is getting real polite before he cuts my throat. He thin-smiled. "I m'be a *gringo* but I ain't a green one. The money is locked up in the Laredo Bank," he lied. "I'll settle up with you when you hand the first herd over. Bein' that you know the territory you pick where you want to bring the cattle over. Me and my boys will be waitin'. If you're happy with the price and I'm likewise about the cattle, why then we'll have a good business goin' on between us. Both of us making good money."

Helman waited for Carlos's answer. He couldn't read it in the bandit leader's face but he reckoned that Carlos was trying his damnedest to think of some way he could double-cross the *gringos* and finish up with all the cake, and still be alive to enjoy it.

"That's a better way of conductin' business than sittin' here on our asses wastin' valuable time gettin' drunk on rotgut whiskey," he said. "And chancin' that things might get out of hand between my boys and yours. Why, if you get things movin' real speedy-like you could have my first payout in your hands before we got sobered up enough to get back on to our horses. Then your *muchachos* can have all the liquor they can down."

Carlos took a final look at the *gringos'* rifles still held in their hands, then at Helman. The *gringo* leader was a man like him, a *mal hombre*, a bad-ass. He and his Texicans were men not easily surprised. The only way he could get money from Helman without any bloodshed was to go along with his deal. Reluctantly he forced his face to dissolve into a make-believe smile.

"*Amigo*," he said, putting out his hand, "we have a deal."

"*Bueno*," replied Helman, sealing the deal by gripping Carlos's hand with his own. "Perole can stay with you then when you're ready to move the cattle he can let me know, I'll be roomin' in Laredo." Helman turned to his men. "OK boys, break camp. Let's get back across the river and get ourselves some drinkin' and whorin' time in. We've got some heavy work ahead of us for the next few months and all you'll be gazin' at are Longhorns' asses."

11

WOODROW felt that his luck was riding high, Helman's trail was still warm. Point riders of one of the many herds trailing north to the Kansas railhead towns told him of how a bunch of ten, twelve riders passed them heading south. Riders, they opined, who were trail-hands returning from driving their bosses' cattle to Kansas. Woodrow confidently knew otherwise.

"It looks as though they are headin' for Mexico, Blue Duck," Woodrow said.

"We're only a couple days ride from the Rio Grande," Blue Duck said. "I could ride on ahead, check things out. Helman could have made camp this side of the river."

Blue Duck's suggestion made sense, Woodrow thought. Round any bend in the trail, this close to him, he could stumble, unprepared, into Helman's camp. "You do that, Blue Duck," he said. "Me and Mr Lewis will make camp here. Give us time to rest the horses, and me. I ain't been up on a horse since I don't know when."

★ ★ ★

It had been five days since Blue Duck had left on his scouting expedition and Woodrow resting up against a tree began to fear for his safety. How would Belle take it if he had to tell her that she was once more on her own? He reckoned that she was hard-bitten enough to take it in her stride. She already knew that taking up friendships with men who earned their keep outside the law couldn't be relied on to be long-living. Cal's cry of, "Rider comin' in, looks like Blue Duck!" got him hurriedly to his feet, glad that Belle wouldn't have to be looking around for another man to share her bed with.

Woodrow was man enough to admit that first impressions of a man can sometimes be dead wrong. On his first clapping eyes on Blue Duck he had labelled him as a shifty-eyed, untrustworthy character. Now, as Blue Duck dismounted and came towards him he seemed somehow more forked-tongue-visaged. Charitably Woodrow put it down to Blue Duck's natural-bred, pinched-ass disposition, like some men who are born smilers, but for some unexplained reason it set his warning nerves on edge, which didn't incline him any more favourably to Blue Duck than he had been when he had left Younger's Bend.

"Any joy?" he asked.

Blue Duck nodded. "I don't exactly know where Helman is now but talk has it by men who have contacts across in Mexico that a bunch of *gringos* is expected soon to pick up a herd of stolen Yankee beef at Buffalo Wallow wash. They've done a deal with a Mex *bandido* called Carlos. The *gringos* they spoke of might not be Helman and his boys but it wouldn't harm us none if we were to make a trip to the wash and see who shows up."

Woodrow grunted with satisfaction. It could only be Helman. He'd had more luck than he had dared hoped for. He was almost within shooting distance of Helman and Perole. Now, he thought, came the hard part, to put paid to the two sons-of-bitches and get hold of the money they must be carrying. He could pick out a nice spot on the trail and bushwhack them when they were driving the herd from the Rio Grande. It would be like shooting fish in a barrel as they would be fully occupied keeping the herd bunched up and on the move. Though that would not get him the money, unless he shot the ten men Helman had with him. A small massacre that would have every lawman in Texas chasing after him, and Cal. Not that the kid would back him up in the shooting, Woodrow dismissed that plan of action almost as soon as he had dreamed it up. Helman would have had no qualms in gunning down any number of men if it brought him riches, but he prided himself that he hadn't slipped that far down the lawless scale to carry out cold-blooded killings. It was, he concluded, wait-and-see time. Play it as it came up.

"You've done OK, Blue Duck," he said. "Rest up a spell then you can ride back to Younger's Bend. It's mine and Mr Lewis's quarrel from now on in."

"I'll stay and tag along with you, Mr Liddell," Blue Duck said. "There's a heap of them and only two of you. And Belle would want me to help you out all I could."

"Why that's mighty brotherly of you, Blue Duck," replied Woodrow. "It would be downright foolish of me to turn down another gun. Ain't that so, Mr Lewis?"

Cal was a long way from thinking it so. Like Woodrow he had become no friendlier towards Blue Duck on their long ride across Texas. He couldn't understand Mr Liddell's reasoning in taking Blue Duck on. The old goat had told him to keep an eye on Blue Duck and now he had the chance to get rid of the weasel-eyed son-of-a-bitch he was welcoming him to stay on with open arms. He'd had little enough sleep as it was watching Blue Duck all hours. It looked as though his cat-nap sleeping was going to continue.

In spite of Cal's misgivings, Woodrow knew what he was doing. He had seen a hungry-for-money look flash across Blue Duck's face when he asked if he could stay with them. The sneaky bastard had cooked up something while he had been scouting along the Rio Grande. Something, he could feel in his old owlhoot bones, not to his or the kid's benefit. If he was right it was better to keep Blue Duck where he could see him, be able to shoot him if necessary. It was sounder, and safer, tactics than letting him ride off to do whatever mischief he had in his mind when his and Cal's guard was down. They broke camp, Blue Duck riding point again, allowing Woodrow to pass on another warning to Cal. "Watch him real close, Mr Lewis," nodding his head in the direction of Blue Duck. "I've more than a strong feelin' that that *hombre* is all set to jump us."

Cal wondered if he should tell Mr Liddell that he had never shot at anything bigger than a four-legged varmint before. He consoled himself with the thought that a man who would double-cross his trail buddies was lower than a varmint.

Blue Duck, broke into a confident grin. The old fart didn't suspect a thing. He had been telling the truth to Woodrow about Helman. He wanted Woodrow as near to Helman's whereabouts as he could before he made his move against him. Then it would be less distance to lead a horse with a dead man strapped across its back, or a man tied up tight on it.

One way or another Blue Duck was going to take Liddell to Helman. What disagreement there was between the two of them didn't matter to him but he reckoned that Helman would owe him if he presented him a man who was hunting him down. Dead or alive Liddell would be his in to join Helman's gang. The kid, he thought, had rubbed him the wrong way the first time he had seen him; it would give him great pleasure to plug him just for the hell of it.

Blue Duck was keen to join up with Helman but that eagerness hadn't made him think foolishly, think that he was better than he was. Two men were one too many for him to jump. Especially when one of them was a man who had lived by the gun long before he was born. In fact he wanted it to appear that he had no part in the forthcoming ambush. Three against two were odds he didn't favour either. If it came to gunplay no matter how many men were backing him up he would be the sole target for Liddell's gun, even if the old bastard was drawing his last breath. He intended to look as alarmed and shocked as Liddell and the kid would when the two men he had hired stepped in the clearing and threw down on them. The bushwhacking of a man like Woodrow Liddell was not without risks, but, he broodingly thought, it was worth taking if it meant kissing goodbye to Younger's Bend and that old domineering bitch, Belle Starr.

They were part way along a brush and tree-lined stretch of the trail when from either side of the trail a man stepped out, covering them with rifles.

"Hold it there, pilgrims," one of the riflemen said. "And don't go for your guns or we'll blow you clear out of your saddles."

Blue Duck grabbed for air with both hands. Woodrow and Cal slowly raised their arms sideways, well away from their bodies. Woodrow fierced-eyed the two bushwhackers and silently, but profanely, cursed Blue Duck. It could have been treachery on his part, he thought, to have been caught by the balls. He was in no doubt that the two men hadn't just stumbled on them riding along the trail. Woodrow knew all about bushwhacking and this was slick, and planned for. The same thoughts were passing through Cal's mind and he was too riled-up at Blue Duck double-crossing them to be scared.

"Pistols and rifles out, slow and easy like and sling them this way," came the barked order from the same man.

"Do as the asshole says, Mr Lewis," said Woodrow, his cold-eyed look still boring in on the two ambushers.

Rifles and pistols thudded in the dust.

"Now you, Grandpa, step down," said the talking man. "Keep a bead on the other two, Sam, while I hog-tie the old fart."

Blue Duck lowered his arms. Things were going smoothly, there was no longer any need for pretence. He reckoned it was gloating time. He swung his horse round and faced Woodrow. Sneering he said, "You ain't so smart as you thought you were, old man, are you?"

"Blue Duck," Woodrow said, conversationally, "I rightly figured you as a possible double-dealin' sonuvabitch the first time I saw you sittin' on Belle's stoop. Though I'll admit I didn't know what lowdown trick you'd come up with."

Blue Duck's face worked in anger. "Get the bastard roped up!" he snarled.

Woodrow, sideways on to the two riflemen as he swung out of his saddle, blocking their view, yanked out the shotgun from his bedroll, and pushed himself away from his horse. As his feet touched the ground he twisted round and with shotgun held across his belly, fired off both barrels.

The right-hand bushwhacker caught the full blast of one barrel, thrusting him backwards as though buffeted by a sudden gust of wind before he fell to the ground, face and upper chest torn and bloodied. His *compadre* only got part of the second barrel, low in the stomach, though enough to send him with one piercing scream of pain along the road to hell.

Blue Duck sat frozen in his saddle, wondering how his fortunes could change for the worst so quickly as he gazed, mesmerized like a rabbit facing a rattler, at the muzzle of a big pistol that Liddell had pulled out from somewhere. He felt the warm wet of his piss spreading across his thighs and was too scared to be embarrassed at who noticed his shame.

"It . . . it wasn't my intention to see you hurt, Mr Liddell," the words coming out in a fear dry-throated stammer.

"Yeah, I just bet you weren't," Woodrow said, scathingly. "You were just goin' to deliver me all wrapped up to the nearest state marshal in the hope that there were papers out on me and collect any reward that may be due. If I'd put up a fight it wouldn't have put you out none to take me in dead." Woodrow beady-eyed the silent-tongued Blue Duck for several seconds then reading something in his face he said, "Why you lowdown sonuvabitch, you were intendin' handin' me over to Helman, weren't you?"

Blue Duck, still tight-mouthed, ass-shuffled nervously in his saddle. And Woodrow knew that he had guessed right.

"Have you told Helman I'm on his trail?" he asked.

"No . . . no, Mr Liddell, I ain't," Blue Duck said, finding his voice, the words babbling out like an hysterical girl's cries. "I thought that if I took you to him he'd let me join up with him. But I ain't seen him, I swear on my mother's grave I ain't had contact with him. And it's the gospel truth about him comin' to the Rio Grande to pick up a herd of beef." Blue Duck looked pleadingly at Woodrow.

"What do you think Helman would

have done to me?" Woodrow snarled. "Hugged me like a long lost brother?" Drawn-faced with anger he put a Colt .44 shell into Blue Duck's right shoulder. Blue Duck howled loud and long and fell across his saddle-horn clutching at his wounded arm, face sickly green and sobbing with pain.

"It's only outa kindness to Belle that I ain't sendin' you along the same road as those two saddle-bums lyin' in the dirt there," Woodrow told him. "Though I reckon if Belle finds out that you were prepared to sell me down the river she'll send you wingin' there herself. Now, I'd strongly advise you to stop your moanin' and ass-kick to the nearest sawbones and get that arm seen to before it goes bad on you."

His face still screwed up with shock and pain Blue Duck heeled his mount into a walk. Woodrow kept his gun in his hand till he disappeared from his sight. He turned and faced Cal. "Let's get these two fellas covered up, Mr Lewis," he said as he reloaded the shotgun and slipped it back into his bedroll.

Mr Lewis didn't want to do anything but throw up. The speed and the matter of factness with which the old man took lives scared him half to death. Mr Liddell was killing them in twos. Though, logically thinking, the old man had had no option to shoot down the men he had seen him kill. And one thing for sure, he would have to get used to sudden and violent death because when Mr Liddell met up with Helman and his boys the amount of killing he had experienced up till now would be small beer compared to the blood that would flow then. And Mr Liddell was relying on him to back him up, do some killing of his own if needs be. Cal felt another wave of sickness coming up from his stomach.

While they put the last few rocks on the double grave Cal asked Woodrow about something that had been bothering him since the shooting. "Why did you not bandage up Blue Duck's wound,

Mr Liddell?" he said. "He could bleed to death before he finds someone to see to it."

"That could be so, Mr Lewis," replied Woodrow. "But Blue Duck chose to get himself shot." Then he looked at Cal as though he had been asked an obviously foolish question that answered itself. "Why if I'd seen to his arm what was to stop the sneaky sonuvabitch doubling back and picking us off at night when we're asleep, eh? If you favour takin' up stage robbin' you'll have to stop thinkin' that foolish, sentimental crap. Think only of number one, or your pard, if you're ridin' with one." Woodrow's lips twitched in a slight humourless smile. "Just remember, Mr Lewis, Blue Duck was only goin' to tie me up. What the hell do you think he had in mind for you, eh?" Woodrow's gaze flickered down to the oblong wedge of rocks. And Cal had to fight real hard to prevent how much he was screwed up inside from showing on his face.

He had read some of Ned Buntline's stories of The Wild Untamed West, where men called each other out; tipping their hats to the ladies they were dallying with in the saloon then walking out into the Main Street to face each other. Each offering the other the chance to draw their pistols first. Buntline, Cal thought, had written a load of crap. He had witnessed men killed and wounded with as much feeling of remorse as a man would easing his ass off a chair to break wind would feel.

"I guess you're right, Mr Liddell," he said.

"You'd better believe it, kid," Woodrow said bluntly. "Then you've a chance to live a heap longer if you do. Now let's get mounted up and head for the Rio Grande."

★ ★ ★

The Rio Grande made a broad sweeping left-hand bend up river of Buffalo

Wallow crossing, slowing it down to a sluggish, unbroken stretch of calm water, the banks on both sides of the river, sandy soil, three or four feet high, gently sloping down to the water's edge. And ideal wetback crossing. Woodrow close-eyed the ground around the *gringo* side of the wash then said, "Ain't no cows stepped this way for several weeks, Mr Lewis." He looked further west along the bank and saw buildings shimmering in the heat haze about a quarter of a mile away. "We'll rest up there to wait for Helman. There's bound to be a *cantina* of sorts in the village. It'll be no grand hotel but it's better than beddin' down in the open. It gets kinda chilly along the river come the early hours. We can get some more stores in, give the horses and gear a good checkin' over." Woodrow pointed over his shoulder. "Herman and his boys will come ridin' in from that direction, that hell's kitchen, Laredo's not far away. I reckon that's where he is. Beyond that village is only desert." He grinned at the doubtful looking Cal. "Even bad-asses don't like to rough it if they don't have to and they've got the money to buy a little comfort such as a warm bed and soft warm women to go with it."

"Might they not be in that village waiting for the cattle to show up at the wash?" Cal said, still not fully convinced of Woodrow's reasoning.

"Ain't likely," replied Woodrow. "Though naturally I don't intend ridin' in without checkin' it out first. But Helman's ridin' around with a parcel of money and he won't want to sit on it this close to the Rio Grande any length of time. The greaser *bandido* he's made the cattle deal with will know he's got money and might take it in his mind to relieve Helman of it. That way he gets to keep the cattle. Deals made along the border ain't as bindin' as those made by slick lawyers in city offices, Mr Lewis." Woodrow looked at the village again. "I wonder if there's any sweet-assed *sēnoritas* who will serve an old *gringo* in there. Belle Starr as old as she is, kid, set my juices flowin' again."

Cal shook his head in amazement. The next few days could be the last on this sweet earth for the old goat and all that seemed to concern him was if there were suitable women in the village for him to hump. Suddenly Cal realized that he had no guarantee of long living ahead of him. He grinned. "M'be there'll be one to suit me, Mr Liddell. I ain't exactly bein' overpowered with woman since I was fully growed up."

Woodrow grinned back at him. "You're learnin', kid; you're learnin' that it don't alter what's comin' to us by frettin' over what ain't happened. Now let's get along to that village while them there can see who we are. Folks in these border villages become kinda nervous at night riders payin' them a call. Could attract us some unwanted lead."

12

"IT is a poor village, *señor*," the old Mexican said. He drew on the makings Woodrow, sitting next to him under the shelter of the *cantina* porch, had given him. "Hard men, *hombres* of my blood and *gringos*, ride along the river line. They come here and take what little we have, food, our women. All without pity and payment. And kill anyone who dares to stop them." The old man turned his head and looked directly at Woodrow. "You are not just an old *gringo*, are you, *señor*?" he said. "The chico who rides with you has still only a boy's face but you have the look of a hard *hombre*." The old man shifted his head to gaze across the smooth expanse of the Rio Grande again. "It is not polite, or indeed wise, to ask men their business, especially an old *gringo* who

167

has the face of a hard *hombre* but I do not think that you and your *compadre* have ridden into San Jose to sit next to an old Mexican." Woodrow saw the old man's deeply etched face crease further in a smile. "Unless you have come to steal Pablo's goats."

"I ain't taken up with goats, alive or as chow, *señor*," Woodrow said. "Though I would have appreciated the delights of a young *cantina señorita* to warm an old man's blood. I hope to have some outstandin' business settled-up with a certain *hombre* whom I'm expectin' to come ridin' this way soon."

The old man caught his eye once more. "Like me, *señor*," he said, "you'll have to make do with the heat of the sun to heat your blood. The girls who have reached the age when men lust after them have left the village to work in the *gringo* whorehouses in Laredo and Del Rio. There they get paid Yankee dollars for what if they stayed in San Jose some *mal hombres* would take for free."

"It smells like chow-time," Woodrow said. "And eatin' is about all we old timers can look forward to nowadays, amigo." Half-smiling he close-eyed the old Mexican for a moment or two then said, "How many unwilling girls did you deflower when you rode the line as a *bandido*, old man?"

The old man showed toothless gums in a high-pitched cackling laugh. "Not so many as to make up for the long years I have sat on this porch all dried up inside like an old nun. How did you know I was once a *bandido, gringo*?"

"It's common knowledge that there are only two kinds of men who live along the border," Woodrow said. "Men who wear lawmen's badges, and the *hombres* they chase. You don't have the pinched-ass look of a badge-toting man." He placed the makings of another five or six cigarettes at the side of the old man before getting on to his feet and going inside the *cantina*.

The *cantina* was a dark, dust-shrouded, two-roomed building. The owner had let the *gringos* use the back room as sleeping quarters. The two cots it held were formerly used by the *cantina* girls to entertain the casual client who passed through San Jose willing to pay for their favours. Cal wasn't impressed with the sleeping arrangements saying that he had smelt sweeter-smelling hogpens.

Woodrow laughed. "The owner has probably just heaved the hogs out so that he can earn himself a few Yankee dollars. But it ain't bad, it's dry and it'll keep the cold wind from us. One time up in Nevada I holed-up nigh on four days in a cave knee-deep in bat shit till the posse who was chasing me got tired of haulin' their horses' asses over the high ridges. Now that, Mr Lewis, was some smell."

Woodrow settled back on the cot, checking over in his mind tasks that needed doing to ensure his and Cal's safety. It didn't do to get too confident just because he had got this close to Helman without any serious mishaps.

It had been serious mishaps for the four men he had shot. This was *bandido* country. The unexpected showing up of Helman and his boys wasn't the only threat they could be facing. A two-bit Mexican gang of cut-throats could ford the Rio Grande and cause them grief. The horses were bedded down out of sight in a part-demolished hut at the rear of the *cantina* and he had paid Pablo, the village goatherd, to inform him of any body of riders approaching the village; day or night. Most urgently if they were *gringos* and riding in from Laredo. Woodrow reckoned that he had everything tied up tight. Though as yet he hadn't figured out just how he was going to tackle Helman and his crew. But, he thought, there was no need for him to get in a sweat over it. Helman had to drive his cattle some place and somewhere along that trail he could possibly get the chance to jump Helman and get what was left of the robbery cash.

That, he opined, would bring a

successful ending to a long trail, the length of the United States of America. For a moment Woodrow wondered how high the tally of dead men would rise before that day. He made sure that the shotgun and one pistol was within easy grabbing distance in the dark, then with a "Good night, Mr Lewis," turned over on to his side and seasoned campaigner that he was, soon dropped off to sleep.

Cal spent a more restless night. He fell asleep thinking of Beth, naked, in all her glory, tantalizingly smiling at him. Then that pleasant picture was shattered by the bloody, ghostly features of men coming at him with pistols blazing, the four men he had seen well and truly shot dead by Mr Liddell. Two he had helped to bury. He woke up with a start, sweating and shivering as though gripped by swamp fever. He was still awake when he saw the new dawn's first light through a hole in the roof of the *cantina*.

★ ★ ★

Pablo, the village goatherd, saw the lone rider coming along the river trail from the direction of Laredo a little after the sun had began to lose its height. Noting that it was only one man approaching San Jose, Pablo didn't think it was worth the effort of getting off his ass and reporting his sighting to the old *gringo*. Besides the *gringo* had told him to be on the lookout for *gringo* riders and this rider he could see as he came nearer was a Mexican 'breed.

Perole, like Woodrow, had given the ground at the crossing a keen examination. He wasn't looking for cattle tracks, but iron-shod hoof tracks. He had suggested to Helman that he should ride to Buffalo Wallow a day or so before the cattle was due to arrive there.

"I ain't runnin' my own kin down, Helman," he said, "but Carlos is the biggest, murderin' thief in Chihuahua.

It's natural thinkin' on his part to try and steal from a *gringo*. To protect our interests it makes sense for me to ride to the Rio Grande before Carlos brings the cattle there to make sure that he don't send some of his boys across early to set up an ambush for us when we're driving the cattle. Carlos would be highly delighted if he could get the money for the cattle and the cattle back."

Helman smiled. "No offence to your kin, Perole, but I already figured that Carlos was a born double-crossing sonuvabitch. You go ahead and scout around. Unless I hear from you otherwise me and the boys will be there as scheduled."

Perole saw recently made tracks of at least five horses near the crossing but that didn't alarm him. They had been made by riders coming down from the north, then he noticed that they hadn't crossed the Rio Grande. Instead they had turned west and headed towards the village further up river. Perole followed their tracks to the village, to spend the night there and to double-check that no bunch of Mexicans had sneaked across the river by asking a few questions of its inhabitants.

There were no horses tied up outside the *cantina* so Perole assumed the tracks he was following were made by drifters or cowhands riding back to their ranch. He hardly glanced at the old Mexican sitting with his back against the *cantina* wall, battered *sombrero* tilted over his eyes. The old man wouldn't have noticed if half the Mexican army had come whooping and splashing over the Rio Grande.

Woodrow, sitting at a table putting his rifle back together again after cleaning and oiling the action, looked up as the light coming through the door was blocked out by a man standing in the opening. He couldn't make out the man's features but the man's loud gasp of, "*Madre de Dios!*" and the quick movement of his right hand to his waist as he jumped back out of sight yelled out who it was. Woodrow moved just as fast. He heaved over the heavy-planked table on to its side and flung himself down behind it just as Perole's pistol shells ploughed into its protecting surface.

Woodrow was between a rock and a hard place. The pieces of his rifle were scattered all over the dirt floor of the *cantina* out of reach, even if he had time to reassemble the rifle. Once Perole saw that he wasn't cutting loose at him he would know that he was unarmed and come into the *cantina* and plug him close up. Woodrow cursed. His long spell of good luck had taken a deep and deadly dive for the worst.

Cal, hearing the shots, left feeding the horses and ran across to the *cantina*, pistol fisted. Once inside he slowed down and cat-footed, strode across to the door and cautiously peered into the bar. He saw Woodrow crouched down behind an upturned table, then he glimpsed a man poke a gun round the front door post and fire at Woodrow.

He waited, all tensed up till the man showed himself again, then gripping his pistol tighter he pulled off two quick loads at him.

It was Perole's turn to do some cursing being temporarily blinded by chips of adobe knocked off the wall by Cal's near misses. As he regained his balance and came to terms with the unexpected fact that Liddell was no longer a sitting duck and that now he had a real gunfight on his hands he stepped on something soft, felt it jerk beneath his feet, and he was off his balance again. This time, cursing more profanely, falling forward through the *cantina* doorway.

As he fell into the *cantina* Cal fired off the remaining loads in his Colt. The three shells drove into Perole's chest stopping his cursing for ever. For a split-second it stopped his falling, raising the top of half of his body higher, long enough for Cal to see the grimacing death-mask of a face, then he continued his downward motion to hit the floor with a dust-lifting thud.

Woodrow was on his feet, running over to Perole, knife in hand, ready to give him the final push through the gateways of hell. He saw with a professional glance that the *coup de grâce* wasn't needed.

"You hit Perole dead centre, Mr Lewis," he said, admiringly. "I couldn't have done a cleaner job myself." More soberly he added, "though I would never have got the chance, the sonuvabitch had me well and truly by the balls. I'm beholden to you, Mr Lewis. He was, in case you ain't guessed, one of Helman's boys."

Cal gave Woodrow a sickly smile at his compliment. He had killed his first man. Though he knew it had been in self-defence, albeit in Mr Liddell's defence, it was something he couldn't make a habit of doing. If he had ever doubted that his attempt at robbing the stage was to be his one and only heist those doubts were gone as he gazed down, still weak-kneed at the man he had killed.

"It wasn't all my doin', Mr Liddell," he said. "I had help. That old Mexican who sits outside played the main part. He gave me Perole on a plate, tripped him up with a piece of cloth."

Woodrow, followed by Cal, walked out of the *cantina*. The old Mexican was just draping his serape back over his shoulders.

"*Muchas gracias, amigo*," Woodrow said. "It could have been real nasty for me in there without your help."

"We old *pistoleros* are a fast-dying breed," the old Mexican said. "I could not watch it dying any faster." He smiled up at Woodrow. "I would be very lonely in my thoughts, *amigo*, sitting here thinking that I was the last of them. We old men have only our memories to comfort us."

"You ain't but right there, amigo," Woodrow said. "But that don't make me any less beholden to you." He turned to Cal. "Now let's get that

179

hombre inside planted well away from here, Mr Lewis, then there'll be no comeback from Helman on the village." Woodrow looked down at the old Mexican once more. "If other *gringos* come here and ask where he is, amigo, tell them that Texas lawmen took him away. Helman will see our horses' tracks so that should convince him that you're tellin' the truth. He won't probe any deeper. He ain't a man to worry or fret too long about the disappearance of one of his men. And that's what we've got to do, Mr Lewis, make ourselves scarce. Helman can't be too far behind Perole."

13

HELMAN dismounted and walked into the *cantina*, expecting to see Perole inside with his hands round a whore, or a bottle of tequila, knowing Perole's strong urges his hands maybe round both at the same time. To his surprise he found the rat hole empty, not even the owner was about the place. Having his siesta somewhere, Helman thought, like the old greaser sitting outside snoring like a pen full of hogs. Helman came outside and kicked the old man in the ribs.

"Hey greaser," he snarled. "I'm lookin' for a 'breed, mounted up on a big black. Should've rode in yesterday."

The old man's lips tightened with pain. He had not been asleep. He had seen the *gringo* entering the village, his eyes still keen enough to see the men who had come with him now waiting at the crossing. He looked at Helman, anger lightening up the backs of his eyes, cursing the fact that he was a stiff-jointed old man. In his younger days if the pig of a *gringo* had so much as given him an unkind look he would have felt the coldness of a knife blade across his throat, then the warmness of blood as his life drained away from him. He prayed that the old *gringo* would make his wish come true.

"The *hombre* you seek was here, *señor*," he said. "But *gringo* lawmen came and took him away."

"Lawmen?" snapped Helman.

"Texas Rangers," replied the old man. Then knowing that the *gringo* pig could have seen the tracks of the old *pistolero* and his *compadre's* horses he added, "Five of them."

The old greaser was speaking the truth, Helman thought. Alongside Perole's tracks leading to the village he had seen the hoof-prints of at least another

182

five horses. Damn him. He had told Perole to go easy on the liquor. Too much tequila turned the 'breed into a prodding man. And hard-assed Texas Rangers weren't the type of men for a Mex 'breed to get uppity with. With Perole gone he would have to do all the contacting with the cutthroat Carlos. And that bastard was an unstable character. His hatred of the *gringos* might come out on top against his love of Yankee dollars. He could well end buried up to the neck in an ant-hill. At least Perole wasn't carrying any of the railroad cash with him. He swung back on to his horse and rode back to the wash. The old Mexican spat in the dust at his going and heaped more curses on his head.

"There's a whole lot of dust bein' raised across the river, boss," one of Helman's men said as he rode up to them. "Too slow movin' to be riders. So it looks like the greasers are on time with your beef."

Helman stood up in his stirrups and

looked across the Rio Grande. "You're right, Slim," he said. "It's the beef. There's too much dust bein' rifted to be anything else." He sat back down in his saddle. "OK boys, you know the drill. If those Mexs try to put one over us, forget the cattle, gun the greasers down."

★ ★ ★

Carlos and his men rode across the Rio Grande ahead of the first of the longhorns entering the water, Carlos still having thoughts of double-crossing the *gringos* till he saw that the *gringo* leader had been reading his mind. He and five of his men were on foot and spread out along the river-bank holding rifles high across their chests. Ideally positioned, he sickeningly felt, to inflict heavy losses on him and his *muchachos* if he tried any tricks, himself, he knew with deadly certainty, being the first target for the *gringo* bullets. The rest of the *gringos*, he saw, were mounted,

184

ready to help to get the herd on to Texas soil. Carlos choked back his disappointment as he drew up his horse in the shallows just short of dry land. Smiling he called out to Helman. "Are they not good cattle, amigo?"

Helman grinned. "I bet the sonuvabitch ain't smilin' inside," he whispered to the man next to him. "Not when he's close-eyein' the Winchesters." Raising his voice he yelled, "They look fine to me, friend. So do the Yankee dollars I'll give you when they are all across the river." Lowering his voice again he said, "M'be the fat pig will finally get the message that if he plays square with me he'll make himself a rich greaser *bandido*."

Carlos glanced nervously over his shoulder. He couldn't see Perole on the Texas bank. Was he with more riflemen behind him? The *gringo* leader was thinking the way he had been. Take what he wanted without payment. His false smile faded away. "I do not see my cousin with you, amigo?" he said.

"He got took by the Texas Rangers," Helman told him. "Now let's get these cows on their way north before the rangers come back this way. I don't want a fight on my hands." He grinned at Carlos. "Let's not me and you waste valuable time wonderin' who's goin' to double-cross who first. We've got a good deal goin' here, for both of us, let's not spoil it by mistrust. You tell me when the next herd is due and I'll be here with the money."

14

WOODROW and Cal trailed Helman and the herd, Woodrow pointing out Helman to Cal as that, "mean-faced sonuvabitch bringin' up the drag." On the fourth day on the trail Woodrow saw that Helman and his crew were riding along more relaxed. Not looking over their shoulders so often. Feeling, Woodrow opined, that they had put enough ground between them and the Rio Grande and the possiblity of Mexican bandits jumping them to take the longhorns back. Being a thief Woodrow knew that thieves, unless they're kin, didn't make good business partners. He also thought that it was time he made his move against Helman. He couldn't expect the kid to tag along with him much longer. And they were running short of supplies.

Woodrow had to accept the unpalatable fact that the likelihood of ever tracking down Zeb and Stu was practically non-existent. The only man left who could tell him where they were was Helman. That meant taking Helman alive and making him talk. That, thought Woodrow, was real crazy thinking, putting his thirst for vengeance before his and Mr Lewis's safety. He would have to be satisfied with getting hold of the money that he reckoned would be in Helman's saddle-bags, then have the pleasure of shooting Helman when the opportunity came up that didn't jeopardize him and the kid. He would send Mr Lewis on his way before that event.

He intended shooting Helman at long range, where there couldn't be any witnesses. The kid wasn't hard enough to take that kind of action. He could think that it was murder to even kill a murderer without a trial by a judge and jury and think badly of him. That would upset him as he had grown fond of the kid. He had proved himself a real pardner, came through with flying colours at San Jose.

Woodrow noted the activity at the camp, the night riders, three of them, going out to nurse the herd, and the rest of the crew settling down for the night around the fire. More importantly for his plan he saw the horses, tethered in a grab of cottonwoods, well back out of the light from the fire. He sat and watched the camp as silent and unmoving as an Indian. The talking had stopped as the men began laying out their bedrolls, pulling them closer to the fire that was beginning to die down. There would never be a better time for what he had in mind, he thought. He got to his feet and walked across to Cal huddled up in his blanket asleep. He shook him awake.

"Are you still with me, Mr Lewis?" he asked.

"With you, what do you mean, Mr Liddell?" Cal said sharply, not too happy at being woken up to be asked

189

a dumb question.

"Are you still my pard?" Woodrow said.

Cal briefly wondered if the old man had finally gone *loco*. Here he was trying to get to sleep on hard ground, having his balls frozen off in a cold camp when the old man wakes him up just to ask him if he was still his pard. "I said I was back at Younger's Bend, remember?" he replied. "Now let me get back to sleep, if I can."

"Good," said Woodrow. "Good I mean about being my pard, but you ain't goin' back to sleep." He bared his teeth in a wolf's fearful grin. "We are goin' to pay Helman a visit."

★ ★ ★

Cal slowly belly-crawled through the brush. Raising his head he could see the deeper darkness of the trees silhouetted against the backdrop of a cloudless, starlit sky he was making for. He had heard that rattlers didn't normally hunt at night, but he couldn't see one taking kindly to him if he rolled on it. Night-time or not it would naturally bite the hell out of him for being woken up.

Once he reached the edge of the timber he stood up thankfully. Still silently and slowly he moved from tree to tree, shielding himself from any watchful eyes at the camp, till he was near enough to hear the snorting and wind-breaking of the horses. Four trees on he could smell them. He had heard no shouts of alarm or gunshots from the direction of the camp whose fire was just a dim red glow through the trees to his left so he assumed that Mr Liddell was in position waiting for him to start the ball.

"You spook the horses, Mr Lewis," he had said. "That should get the bastards jumpin' off their blankets pretty damn quick. The time it takes them to round up the horses should be long enough for me to get the cash from Helman's saddle-bags. But if you hear any ruckus goin' on at the camp it means I'm in the shit. That don't mean you've got to come fire-ballin' in to pull me out of it, Mr Lewis. You come back here and pick up your gear and ass-kick it out of the territory. If I can I'll meet up with you at Younger's Bend. Though if you want to keep on ridin' you do so, understand?"

Cal waited till he was sure that no guard had been posted at the horse lines before he stepped in close enough to be able to touch the end horse. He loosened the holding rope then jabbed the first three horses in their flanks with his knife. The animals reared and squealed with pain and sent a shock wave of panic among the rest of the horses. Kicking and bucking they broke out of the line, scattering through the trees.

Woodrow, face kissing the dirt, within five, six paces of the camp, heard the noise of the horses crashing their fear-driven way through the trees. He grinned into the dirt. The kid was proving his worth again. Then the alarm was raised at the camp. Men were leaping to their feet, yelling, bumping into each other as they pulled on their boots.

"Get the horses!" he heard Helman yell out and in no time at all the camp was deserted as the men hared off after the stampeding horses.

Still hugging the ground Woodrow cleared the last few feet to where Helman's saddle-bags lay. He speedily loosened the straps on one of the bags, reached inside, but could feel no thick wads of money, just clothes. The other bag likewise held no money. "Shit!" Woodrow said bitterly, as he refastened the bags. He had risked his and the kid's neck for damn all. What galled him most as he backtracked his way through the brush was that if he had thought logically about it he ought to have known that Helman wouldn't be riding all over Texas with his saddle-bags bulging with money. Like the stupid asshole he was he had even brought paper and cloths to stuff Helman's bags with so that the son-of-a-bitch wouldn't notice his loss. Keep him feeling confident and easy, till sometime tomorrow when he would draw a bead on him. Ending his vengeance trail.

He heard the click of a pistol being cocked ahead of him and froze in his tracks. Holding his jumping nerves in check he said, "It's me, kid." As he spoke he drew out his own gun with a hand that trembled slightly just in case it wasn't Mr Lewis holding a pistol on him. Liddell, he told himself, you're getting too old for this thieving caper. You're shaking like a virgin on her wedding night. Then he heard the kid answering him with, "Did you get the money, Mr Liddell?"

"No I didn't," he said when he came alongside Cal. "You did well, kid. It was my end that didn't work out right. Helman hadn't the damn money with him, and it was foolish of me not to have realized that. My dumb-thinking put us both in unnecessary danger. I owe you an apology, Mr Lewis."

"Where is the money then?" Cal asked.

"It'll be stashed away somewhere in Laredo I reckon," replied Woodrow. "Helman won't put it in a bank vault. He won't risk showin' his face inside a bank in case a guard or a teller recognizes him as a fella who robs banks."

"What do you intend doin' now, Mr Liddell?" asked Cal. "Shoot Helman as you said and forget about the money?"

Woodrow hard-eyed Cal. "No, I ain't forgettin' about the money. It belongs to me. I'll have to hang around trailin' him till he heads back to Laredo to pick up more cash for another bunch of longhorns from his Mex connections."

Cal could buy Mr Liddell wishing to kill Helman, whatever strong personal reason he had for doing so Helman deserved to pay with his life for his shooting down of the railroad guards. That, he opined was only fair justice, but he thought that the old heister's obsession to get the money was driving him *loco*.

"That could take a while, Mr Liddell," he said.

"I don't think so," Woodrow said. "I've a feelin' that he'll be beddin' down the cows he's drivin' now some place soon. But you needn't stay. You go and pick up that reward money and enjoy spendin' it."

"Well I don't know, Mr. Liddell," said Cal doubtfully. "I made a deal."

"The deal's been paid in full, Mr Lewis," Woodrow said. "I wouldn't be talkin' to you now if it hadn't." He grinned. "A word of advice from an old hand at the game, don't take up heistin' as an occupation you ain't got the temperament for it. And that ain't no reflection on your character."

"I didn't need you to tell me that, Mr Liddell," replied Cal. "I've found out myself that I couldn't hold a pistol on a man and demand his cash then calmly shoot him if he didn't hand it over." Straight-faced he added, "I don't know how I worked myself up to gun down Perole."

Woodrow swallowed hard. He was only just finding out how lucky he had been getting this close to Helman with a whole skin.

"Well whatever," he said gruffly, "you did it, wiped the slate clean between us. So come daylight you ride out and start livin' your own life, OK?"

★ ★ ★

Late afternoon on the day that Cal had left him Woodrow saw the herd being driven off the main trail towards a range of low grassy-topped hills. By nightfall the cattle were grazing in a well-watered blank-ended valley. Near its entrance was a ramshackle-looking soddy. Woodrow thought that it had been a line cabin belonging to a cattle spread that had once run beef across the territory.

Next morning to Woodrow's great relief Helman and six of his men mounted up outside the shack and after a brief conversation with the men who had been left to watch over the herd they set off at a fair pace southwards, Laredo he hoped. And the end of his bone-aching cold-camps. Keeping a safe distance behind them he dogged their trail.

At an equally safe distance behind Woodrow rode Cal, to try somehow to save the old man from his foolishness. Mr Liddell, he opined hadn't a cat in hell's chance of winning through against seven to one odds. Why, he didn't rightly know. As Mr Liddell had said they had saved each other's lives, debts had been honoured on both sides, but Cal had been raised in the belief that there doesn't have to be a reason to do another man a favour if the man involved is a friend.

15

OODROW'S high hopes were realized when he saw Helman and his men cut off the river road and head east to Laredo. There was plenty of traffic on the trail this close to Laredo, freight wagons, stages, and riders coming and going, so there was no danger of Helman thinking suspicious thoughts that he was being trailed by a man he reckoned was dead. Though not wishing to stretch the good luck he was favoured with too far, Woodrow dismounted and left his horses in the care of a Mexican boy living with his parents in a shack on the edge of town, for the price of one silver dollar.

"There's another one when I come back, if you feed and water them," Woodrow said. "Feed's in those bags on the second packhorse." Indian-faced he eyed the small boy. "I'm one *mal hombre*, amigo, if you let any of your ragged-assed *compadres* steal my gear I'll hunt you all down and see you strung up for horse-thievin', savvy?"

The boy boldly grinned up at Woodrow. "I am the *capitan* here, *gringo*, your horses will be safe with me."

"*Bueno*," said Woodrow. And set off on foot to pick up Helman's trail again.

Woodrow was in time to see Helman and his crew come out of a livery barn, shouldering their gear, making for a bar further along the street. His luck was still holding out, he thought. Helman was staying at least one night in Laredo, giving him more time, and a better opportunity, of catching him unawares and getting the money than meeting up with him face to face on the trail backed by his crew. Once they were inside the saloon Woodrow stood under the porch of the barber shop opposite the bar and waited.

Helman and his crew lined the bar, Helman ordering the drinks. "Just two, boys," he said. "No whoopin' it up this visit. Tomorrow we leave for San Jose. Our greaser friend has another bunch of longhorns for us. I've booked you all in at Brophy's rooming-house. It's along the street a piece, past the livery barn. I'll have to push on, I've some business to attend to." He fish-eyed the men bellied up to the bar. "Remember I want all of you sitting up on your horses stone-cold sober when we move out."

Woodrow drew further back under the porch as Helman stepped out of the saloon. He turned left and walked along the boardwalk in the direction he had ridden into town. Woodrow paced him along the street. Helman stopped at a boarded-up building that bore a paint-faded sign that read 'General Store'. Helman, after looking both ways along the street, unlocked the big padlocked door then went inside.

Woodrow gave a gasp of surprise.

Helman's bank. "You sonuvabitch," he breathed. "I never had you figured as an *hombre* overloaded with brains, Helman, but you sure come up with a good idea of where your poke will be safe."

On one side of the empty store was the bank, the other side, the town marshal's office, with the marshal, or one of his deputies, sitting on the porch. Breaking in during the night was out. Fumbling noisily about inside in the dark trying to find where Helman had stashed the money was inviting the law next door to come in wondering why the owner of the store was working with no lights on. No, Woodrow opined, he would have to enter the store legal-like with the key, in the daytime, good day-ing any citizen who came along. That was, of course, after he had relieved Helman of the key with the minimum of fuss, or he would have the law breathing down his neck. Getting hold of the key was going to be something of a problem but to cheer himself up he thought that it wasn't as big as the problems he had faced when he first set out to track Helman down. He had never, in his wildest hopes, expected to get this close to his quarry in so short a time.

Woodrow was man enough to concede that without Mr Lewis's help he wouldn't now be within touching distance of Helman and the money, in fact he would be well and truly dead. Briefly he wondered how the kid was making out and hoped that whatever enterprise he took up with the reward it would make him more money. Helman's going into a rooming-house got Woodrow thinking that Lady Luck was giving him another break. He would give Helman time to get to sleep then Indian up on him and put him into a deeper sleep with the help of the barrel of a Colt and take the key. Before he came to he would be out of Laredo with the money. Then he could lie in wait to honour the promise he made in Canada to put Helman underground.

Cal, not being known to Helman or any of his men, didn't sneak into Laredo the way Woodrow had. He rode boldly in, following Helman and his men into the livery barn, being favoured with cursory, non-interested glances from them. He hung back till they left then trailed them at a slow pace, keeping a watchful eye open for Woodrow whom he knew would be somewhere close by. He spotted him standing on a porch eyeing Helman and his men going into a saloon. He stopped and did some watching of his own.

He saw all that Woodrow had observed; Helman coming out of the saloon, going in and coming out of the empty store and carrying on to the rooming-house. And something Woodrow, staking out the rooming-house, missed. Something that began to nag worryingly at him. As Helman's men were nearing the rooming-house Cal saw one of them look in Woodrow's direction then turn and talk to one of his *compadres*. The same man gave Woodrow another glance before walking up the rooming-house steps. Cal felt like going across to Woodrow to tell him that one of Helman's crew had showed an unusual interest in him but decided against it. If the man who had eyed Mr Liddell, or Helman came out into the street and saw them together Woodrow would lose the only edge he didn't know he had, a back-up man.

Helman was finishing off a meal when his men came into the dining-room.

"You must be wrong, Slim," he heard one of them say as they took their places at the table. "That old bastard died in San Quentin doin' a twenty-year stretch. If he's still alive he must be about a hundred and twenty years old, gaga, in some retirement home for old heisters."

"Well it weren't a ghost I seed standin' on that porch watchin' this place," said Slim. "It was definitely Woodrow Liddell in the flesh. I know him from way back. Helped him to pull off a job once. And I ain't forgot what he looks like."

Helman stiffened up in his chair in alarm, face paling. Liddell? How could the old bastard be here in Laredo when he had shot him dead in a mail car way up in Canada? If Slim had seen right, and it would be dangerously foolish of him not to believe him, how the hell had Liddell tracked him all the way to Laredo? Then he was hit by a sudden gut-churning thought that Perole hadn't been taken by Texas Rangers, it had been Liddell's doing. More disturbing to him was that by the sign he had read in San Jose, Liddell had men to back him up. Helman's gaze flickered nervously towards the door half-expecting to see Liddell bursting in with a bunch of men cutting loose at him.

Slowly his nerves began to settle down as he started to think of ways and means to get out of the situation the unexpected showing up of Liddell had put him in. Why Liddell wasn't dead or how he had picked up his trail was long gone history. Liddell was here, here to get even, see him dead. Which Helman thought was a natural reaction for a man gunned down by a man whom he thought was his partner. He would have done the same. But he reckoned that Liddell was also here to get the money from the robbery. That, he knew for sure, was the only reason he was still alive. Anywhere along the trail to Laredo Liddell could have picked him off with a long gun.

He also accepted that Liddell had seen him go into the store, guessed what was hidden in there. Come dark he would try to break in, or come here to get the key and search for the cash. Yet he still had the edge over Liddell. He would still be thinking that his presence in Laredo had been undetected. Liddell would have to be kept thinking that way. Helman thought for a minute or two then bared his teeth in a cheerless smile. He would use the money to draw Liddell and whoever he had with him into the open where he could arrange an unpleasant surprise for them, finishing off what he had failed to do in Canada.

"Eat up fast, boys," he said. "What Slim's just said means that we've got a bunch of fellas wantin' to muscle in on our cattle dealing. Now that ain't right when we've gone to all the bother and the expense of settin' it up. So I intend to tell the sonsuvbitches just that when we meet up with them. I'll need you, Slim and you, Buz, to help me to get that message across."

★ ★ ★

Through the bar mirror Cal watched Helman's crew playing poker at a table in the back recess of the saloon. He wondered what mischief they were cooking up for Mr Liddell. He had no proof, other than a strong inner feeling that there was more occupying their minds than trying to win the pot. Though there was no reason for the man who had recognized Mr Liddell to have told Helman about it, he wouldn't know that Mr Liddell's purpose in Laredo was to kill his boss, his instincts were telling him that Helman knew that Mr Liddell was outside on the street. He could be wrong, but he wasn't prepared to put his partner's life at risk more than it was now on that chance. As his pa had often told him, forewarned and prepared was like landing the first punch.

On seeing the six men coming out of the rooming-house, Cal, so sure that his reasoning was right, expected them to split up and start seeking Mr Liddell out. To his surprise they kept together and walked back along the street, to the saloon, he opined. He saw that Mr Liddell made no move to follow them, which figured; his business was with Helman. That set him wondering why Helman had not come out on the street with his men. Cal for awhile began to think that his assessment of the whole situation had only been his highly-charged nerves playing him false when the men entered the saloon. Dammit, he said to himself, I am right, the bastards are up to something. He sneaked round the corner of the rooming-house, to keep out of Woodrow's line of vision, then crossing several back lots, he came into the saloon by the rear door. Checking that Helman's crew were still inside, he made his way to the bar.

Slim laid his cards on the table and stood up. "OK, Buzz, Liddell ain't followed us in so let's do it. The rest of you stay here and act normal. If a tall old fart comes in here keep an eye on him. Check out if he's got some boys taggin' along with him."

Cal smiled cock-a-hoop at himself in the mirror as he saw the thin man who knew Mr Liddell and the man he had mentioned it to leave the saloon by the way he had entered. He had been right, he thought grimly. The bastards had got something planned against Mr

Liddell. Quickly he downed his drink and followed them out.

Helman was also making his play. He came out into the street, strode along it like a man who wasn't in a hurry to go any place. Woodrow came alive. Tossing his half-smoked makings away he set off on Helman's trail.

Helman stopped outside the empty store, opened the lock and went inside. When he came out on the porch again with saddle-bags looped over his shoulders Woodrow felt like going to a church meeting-day preaching session and getting on his bended knees to thank whoever it was keeping a kindly eye on him for all the good luck he was blessed with. All that was left for him to do was to stroll across the street, come up behind Helman and jab a gun in his ribs. Then lead him in some quiet alley or empty lot, relieve him of the money before putting a bullet in his treacherous black heart.

Before the alarm was raised that a shootist was at large he would be well out of town, without leaving a hot trail behind him. The marshal on discovering Helman's body would make his first enquiries at the livery barn, asking if anyone had left town hurriedly. It would be quite a spell, Woodrow thought, before the law found out that a Mexican kid had looked after an old *gringo's* horses. An old *gringo* who had left town not long after the dead man was found.

The two men Cal was following came out of the livery barn mounted up on their horses and rode along a narrow trail that Cal opined, led to the Rio Grande. He ran across to the barn and quickly threw his saddle on his horse, then took the same trail as the two men.

Helman was taking all the cash from the store. He had to think the worst, Liddell knowing where the money was. It would be handing it to the old bastard on a plate leaving it there when he rode out to pick up another bunch of cows. He also knew that it was risky carrying all the money with him. Liddell could take it in his head to jump him here in Laredo in broad daylight and chance it ass-kicking it out of town without getting shot. But Helman reckoned it was a calculated risk. To set a good trap you had to have good bait.

The river trail where he had sent Slim and Buz was a quiet trail, the only place Liddell would think that he had a clear-cut chance of taking the money without raising a sweat. He and the money would be the irresistible bait that would lure Liddell, with his tongue hanging out in anticipation, along the trail. Slim and Buz, crouched behind some rocks, were enough fire-power to spring the trap. Even if Liddell came riding along with his boys.

★ ★ ★

Cal noticed the trail ahead of him closing in sharply, funnelling to a narrow, steep-sided cleft bounded on both sides by rock slips. Now he knew the deadly purpose of the two men he was trailing. Even a greenhorn in the back-stabbing business of bushwhacking and drygulching, could see that it was an ideal spot to throw down on an unsuspecting man. Somehow Helman was going to persuade Mr Liddell to walk into the trap. Cal pulled out his rifle and dismounted. Leaving the trail he went forward on foot, stealthily.

He caught the two men off guard, having a smoke before they took up their ambushing positions. He stepped into view, rifle aimed at the taller of the two men. "Just stand nice and easy, gents." Cal ordered. "Or the big fella gets the first one in the guts." He tried to sound like a border tough, hoping that they would not call his bluff.

Slim and Buz stood rock still. Their makings dangling smouldering on slack-jawed lower lips.

"Gunbelts off," Cal said next. "Then you, big fella, get the ropes off the saddles and tie your buddy up real tight with one of them. And no tricks. If you give me as much as an unfriendly look you're dead meat."

★ ★ ★

Woodrow panted and cursed alternately as he leaned against his horse's flank. "Get the saddle on, *pronto, mucho pronto*, amigo," he gasped. "Never mind the packhorses." He tossed the Mexican boy a dollar piece. He had never been so close to the money since he had first gazed on it in the railroad safe, yet it might as well still be in the safe as far as getting hold of it was concerned. He couldn't get near to Helman for all the citizens crowding the boardwalks. Now the bastard was up on his horse riding out of town, causing him to dash here to get his horse as though his ass was on fire.

★ ★ ★

For once Woodrow's owlhoot's sixth sense that warned him of impending danger, failed him. Or his keenness to get within sighting distance of Helman once more had made him deaf to any warning signals. He caught up with Helman sooner than he expected, totally unprepared for the confrontation. Helman sat easily in his saddle at the mouth of a small canyon, greeting him with a swamp 'gator-type smile spying its next meal. Woodrow swore. It was turning out to be a real cursing day for him.

"I'll say this for you," Helman said. "For an old man you sure take some killin'. Don't go for your gun, I ain't alone." Helman raised his voice. "Show yourselves, boys."

Woodrow glanced to his left and saw the tip of a hat and a hand holding a rifle showing from behind a big rock. There was no reason to doubt Helman's word there was another man, likewise armed, on the other side of him.

"I arranged this meeting; one of my boys spotted you in Laredo." Helman continued. "I figured you'd come runnin' if I waved the cash bags in front of you. I want to know how many men are tailin' me before I plug you."

Woodrow favoured Helman with a drop-dead look and remained tight-lipped. He was too busy cursing himself for walking into Helman's trap with his eyes open to be talkative.

Helman close-studied Woodrow for a minute or two then said, "Why you old goat, you're on your own, ain't you?"

Woodrow still kept his peace.

"But who the hell was with you at San Jose?" snapped Helman. "I picked up five sets of hoof-prints there." He gimlet-eyed Woodrow. "An' an old greaser there told me that Texas Rangers had taken Perole. My guts tell me that you shot him."

"There was only me and Blue Duck, Belle Starr's man, and three pack animals," lied Woodrow. If Helman

217

wanted revenge for the death of Perole, the dirty-dealing Blue Duck couldn't be a better candidate. "He left me at San Jose to ride back to Younger's Bend." Woodrow smiled at Helman. "I sure surprised Perole. I was hopin' to do the same to Stu and Zeb before I came and sorted you out. But life's full of disappointments."

Helman switched on his humourless, toothy smile again. "It ain't worth frettin' any more, old man, you're on your way out. You ain't goin' to plug me, that's for sure, and even if you had any livin' ahead of you, you couldn't get even with Stu and Zeb. Those wild assholes got themselves killed in a saloon shoot-out in KC."

Woodrow allowed himself another smile. "I'm more than a mite put out that I didn't down the assholes but they're dead so they'll not be enjoyin' the fruits of their double-cross and that's all that matters."

Helman's face twisted in anger. "Talkin' time is over, old man, it's killin' time now . . . "

"No it ain't, Mr Helman," Cal said, stepping clear of the rocks, his rifle covering Helman. "Just stay easy while Mr Woodrow does some talkin'. You've said your piece."

Helman's hand that was reaching for his gun hung indecisively in mid-air, the anger in his face slowly replaced by a look of incredulous fear. Cal smiled at him. "It ain't any good hopin' that Slim's buddy will help you out. He's all trussed up as tight as Slim is. It's your play now, Mr Liddell."

"You're damn right it's my play, Mr Lewis," Woodrow almost shouted as he let loose his bottled-up rage at being caught short. "And enough time's been wasted yappin'. As that sonuvabitch said, it's killin' time." Woodrow's hand sped for his gun.

A fierce-smiling Helman beat him to the draw. Woodrow's fleeting thought was that he had overreached himself going up against young guns. Helman after all was going to get the pleasure of killing him. Helman's speed was his downfall. His first shot fired without true aim smashed into Woodrow's left arm, the second shell came closer to the target, ripping a furrow across Woodrow's ribs. Then he had run out of time and life for a third shot. Fighting hard to hold back his pain to keep his hand steady, Woodrow pulled off a single shot that hit Helman clean between the eyes, a killing shot, lifting Helman inches out of his saddle before falling forward across his horse's neck. As dead as Perole, Stu and Zeb. Woodrow, grey-faced with pain reholstered his pistol and sagged back in his saddle.

"You young sonuvabitch," he said affectionately as Cal came up to him. "That's twice you've saved my dirty hide." Painfully he grinned. "And I nearly put a slug in you that day you tried to rob the stage. Why did you come back?"

Po-faced Cal said, "I knew that for an old man you were takin' on more than you could handle trackin' down Helman on your own but bein' a cantankerous old bastard you wouldn't take a tellin' so I tagged along to see if I could help." He grinned up at Woodrow. "Now step down and I'll tend to that hand before you become a bigger burden to me by bleedin' to death and forcing me to sweat my balls off seein' you planted."

Woodrow heaved himself out of his saddle. "It's nice for an old fart to know he's thought well of," he said.

★ ★ ★

Slim and Buz had been released, Helman strapped face down across his horse, ready for his last trip to Laredo. Woodrow eyeballed Slim and Buz. "Now you two *hombres* ain't thinkin' of stickin' the law on us when you take your late, unlamented boss back to town, are you? You saw it was a fair fight, fairer than your boss intended. I reckon that you must be upset at suddenly gettin' your pay cut off but think of the money you could make if you push the cattle, who ain't got an owner now, on to Kansas."

Slim looked at Buz as if seeking in his *compadre's* face acceptance of the decision he was about to make. Then he looked at the mean-eyed Woodrow, and at the dead Helman, and quickly made up his mind whether Buz would agree with him or not. "Me and Buz were hired to move cattle not to take on greaser *bandidos* who gunned down our boss before we could do anything to help him, Mr Liddell. But the least we can do is to see that he gets a prayer said over him before he's put under." Slim would dearly have liked to have known what was in the bulging saddle-bags now lying across Liddell's horse. He opined that they were partly responsible for the shoot-out but he thought it would be wiser, and healthier, for him not to be so nosey.

Woodrow favoured him with a

beaming smile. "I reckon we're still friends then so we'll go our different ways. Don't let those eastern dudes in Kansas cheat you out of a fair price for your longhorns."

★ ★ ★

Woodrow and Cal swung around Laredo to pick up Woodrow's packhorses, then, after putting a good two hours' ride between them and Laredo, Cal suggested that they should make camp so that he could boil up some water and clean up the wounds more thoroughly than he had done at the canyon. He got no disagreement from Woodrow whose hand and ribs were giving him hell and who was finding out fast, and painfully, he was an over-the-hill old man.

Resting as comfortably as he could against a tree Woodrow idly watched Cal building up the campfire. He suddenly sat up with a jerk as he saw Cal using some of the money from the robbery instead of kindling to get the fire flaming.

"Jesus Christ! What the hell are you doin'! Have you gone loco?" he cried. He tried to pull his pistol out with his left hand only to find himself staring at the muzzle of Cal's cocked pistol levelled at his face.

"What the hell do you think I'm doin'?" replied Cal. "I'm burnin' the money, the whole damned lot of it."

Woodrow glared angrily, and helplessly at his hard-faced pardner. The kid didn't look like a kid any more. He sure had read him wrong.

"Burn it! What the hell for!" Woodrow said angrily. "Why . . . why it's sacrilege burnin' all that money. Take it all if you want to, but don't burn it!" Groaning he fell back against the tree painfully scowling at Cal.

"Just take it easy, pardner," Cal said soothingly, "It ain't the end of the world you're witnessin'. And I'm doin' it for your sake."

Woodrow gave a derisive snort. "I just bet you are, pardner."

"You told me, and I believed you, Mr Liddell," Cal said, "that you had nothin' to do with the killin' of those guards, but this money has their blood on it. It's tainted money and I want no part of it. Killin' Helman and Perole, and knowin' that the other two fellas who double-crossed you are dead, I reckon settles the wrong they did you. You only did to them what the law would have dished out to them if they'd been caught. By takin' the money you're no better than Helman." He saw Woodrow opening his mouth to protest and raised a hand to shut him up. "OK then," he said. "You didn't actually shoot down the guards but you're willin' enough to take a killer's loot. By not takin' it you've got a chance to end your life as a heister. A chance to settle down some place where you don't have to keep lookin' over your shoulder in case a posse is closin' in on you."

Woodrow gave a bitter laugh. "Settle down? What with? Who'd give an old fart like me paid work?"

"You don't have to look for work, Mr Liddell," replied Cal. "Me and you are pards, remember? And I've got that reward money comin' to me. That should grubstake us to take up some money-makin' business. A small cattle spread, a holdin', m'be a store, I dunno. Something a durn sight better than robbin' trains and stages."

Woodrow looked long and hard at Cal before he answered him. The kid was speaking words of wisdom. His wounds were aching like hell, making him feel as old as Methuselah. Too old to stay alert all day and night in case the law jumped him. He grinned inwardly. What lawman would link an old sodbuster or storekeeper with the notorious heister, Woodrow Liddell.

"Why would you do what you said for me, Mr Lewis?" Woodrow asked. "It ain't that we're kin."

"Why?" replied Cal. "I've just told you why, we're pards." He grinned. "Besides I need an old goat like you to keep me in check or I'll spend all that reward money in the whorehouses."

"Well, burn the damn stuff then, pard," Woodrow growled. "I'm too bushed to argue with you any longer. But don't get upset if you see your pard sheddin' tears. Old habits take a while in dyin'."

THE END

FIGHTING RAMROD
Charles N. Heckelmann

Most men would have cut their losses, but Frazer counted the bullets in his guns and said he'd soak the range in blood before he'd give up another inch of what was his.

LONE GUN
Eric Allen

Smoke Blackbird had been away too long. The Lequires had seized the Blackbird farm, forcing the Indians and settlers off, and no one seemed willing to fight! He had to fight alone.

THE THIRD RIDER
Barry Cord

Mel Rawlins wasn't going to let anything stand in his way. His father was murdered, his two brothers gone. Now Mel rode for vengeance.

ARIZONA DRIFTERS
W. C. Tuttle

When drifting Dutton and Lonnie Steelman decide to become partners they find that they have a common enemy in the formidable Thurston brothers.

TOMBSTONE
Matt Braun

Wells Fargo paid Luke Starbuck to outgun the silver-thieving stagecoach gang at Tombstone. Before long Luke can see the only thing bearing fruit in this eldorado will be the gallows tree.

HIGH BORDER RIDERS
Lee Floren

Buckshot McKee and Tortilla Joe cut the trail of a border tough who was running Mexican beef into Texas. They stopped the smuggler in his tracks.

BRETT RANDALL, GAMBLER
E. B. Mann

Larry Day had the choice of running away from the law or of assuming a dead man's place. No matter what he decided he was bound to end up dead.

THE GUNSHARP
William R. Cox

The Eggerleys weren't very smart. They trained their sights on Will Carney and Arizona's biggest blood bath began.

THE DEPUTY OF SAN RIANO
Lawrence A. Keating and
Al. P. Nelson

When a man fell dead from his horse, Ed Grant was spotted riding away from the scene. The deputy sheriff rode out after him and came up against everything from gunfire to dynamite.

FARGO: MASSACRE RIVER
John Benteen

The ambushers up ahead had now blocked the road. Fargo's convoy was a jumble, a perfect target for the insurgents' weapons!

SUNDANCE: DEATH IN THE LAVA
John Benteen

The Modoc's captured the wagon train and its cargo of gold. But now the halfbreed they called Sundance was going after it . . .

HARSH RECKONING
Phil Ketchum

Five years of keeping himself alive in a brutal prison had made Brand tough and careless about who he gunned down . . .